Prai

"Jenny Hale writes touching, beautiful stories."—**RaeAnne Thayne, *New York Times* bestselling author**

"I can always count on Jenny Hale to sweep me away with her heartwarming romantic tales."—**Denise Hunter, bestselling author,** on *Butterfly Sisters*

One of "19 Dreamy Summer Romances to Whisk you Away" in **Oprah Magazine** on *The Summer House*

One of "24 Dreamy Books about Romance" in **Oprah Daily** on *The Summer House*

Included in "Christmas Novels to Start Reading Now" in **Southern Living Magazine** on *The Christmas Letters*

"Touching, fun-filled, and redolent with salt air and the fragrance of summer, this seaside tale is a perfect volume for most romance collections."—**Library Journal** on *The Summer House*

"Hale's impeccably executed contemporary romance is the perfect gift for readers who love sweetly romantic love stories imbued with all the warmth and joy of the holiday season."—**Booklist** on *Christmas Wishes and Mistletoe Kisses*

Books By Jenny Hale

The Golden Hour

The Magic of Sea Glass

Butterfly Sisters

The Memory Keeper

An Island Summer

The Beach House

The House on Firefly Beach

Summer at Firefly Beach

The Summer Hideaway

The Summer House

Summer at Oyster Bay

Summer by the Sea

A Barefoot Summer

Meet Me at Christmas

The Christmas Letters

A Lighthouse Christmas

Christmas at Fireside Cabins

Christmas at Silver Falls

It Started with Christmas

We'll Always Have Christmas

All I Want for Christmas

Christmas Wishes and Mistletoe Kisses

The
Noel
Bridge

The
Noel
Bridge

JENNY HALE

USA TODAY BESTSELLING AUTHOR

HARPETH ROAD
PRESS®
Nashville

HARPETH ROAD PRESS

Published by Harpeth Road Press (USA)
P.O. Box 158184
Nashville, TN 37215

Paperback: 978-1-963483-11-6
eBook: 978-1-963483-10-9

The Noel Bridge: An Uplifting, Heartwarming Christmas Romance

Cover Design by Kristen Ingebretson
Cover images © Shutterstock

First printing: October 2024

Chapter One

Alicia Silver wiped a tear from her cheek as she sat in her favorite nook, staring out at the morning light. The cushioned window seat had been *the* selling point of the second-floor condo—for her, at least— and the spot that had always soothed her.

Now, nothing could.

Over the last nine months, she'd been lost somewhere between the now and the never—what she called "the gap," an empty void she couldn't climb out of. In the "now", she was nestled alone against the large glass pane. Freezing rain hit the Christmas lights on the palmettos that dotted the edge of the sidewalk. The scene blurred before she squeezed her tired eyes shut, the "never" still haunting her. Her life with the man she'd promised to marry having evaporated, she'd never know that innocent happiness again, never peer down at children who looked like her fiancé, Bo Callahan.

The wind howled in protest of the colder-than-usual temperatures so far south. Georgia residents weren't used to so much ice. But the bad weather was par for the course lately. She tightened the fleece blanket around her shoulders and pulled her knees up to cocoon herself in warmth as she tried to fixate on the present, even though she wasn't sure why she needed to.

Bo's parents, Delia and Bert, had asked her to come over, but she couldn't stomach being around people who'd known Bo so well. Perhaps she should have accepted their invitation. After only one isolating day of her holiday vacation, she prayed for someone—anyone—to walk out the door of the shop below her condo, just to assure her she wasn't alone on this desolate Sunday. She was acutely aware of her solitude, struggling to sleep through the night, the silence constantly reminding her no one was there.

In the center of Savannah, Alicia's condo was situated above a usually vibrant row of merchants. The store just below her sold eclectic housewares. At any other time of year, the sidewalks would be bustling with tourists, locals, or students from Savannah College of Art and Design. Usually, a constant stream of people darted to and fro, jostling their armfuls of shopping bags. They clustered on corners as they waited for traffic to clear so they could cross to the other side of Broughton Street, where they'd continue their retail therapy.

Instead, this weekend the empty streets mirrored her state of mind. And even if people had been outside, a jovial scene wouldn't have alleviated the seclusion Alicia felt.

Unable to manage the bleak atmosphere any longer, she stood and padded across the cement floors of her warehouse-style condo that Bo had always liked more than she had. Ignoring the idle chatter of the television, she clutched the fleece blanket Bo had cuddled up with whenever he was over. She wadded it tightly in her fists and inhaled deeply,

2

knowing she shouldn't. It would only sharpen her crippling grief to take in his lingering scent.

They'd met in her junior year of college and, after four years of dating, he'd asked her to marry him. *For better or worse.* Well, she was worse right now without him and needed him to comfort her. He'd always promised to help her through anything. Yet all she had now was emptiness, the void of him. His things were still there, as if he would walk through the door any minute, but the marker in the cemetery across town reminded her he never would again.

"I knew this would happen." Those had been Bo's first words to her. She'd been sitting at a bar with her friends one night, and he'd come up behind her and whispered them in her ear.

She'd turned around, eyeing the stranger with dark hair and striking features. *"Knew what would happen?"* she'd asked.

"I didn't want to come out tonight, but my friends convinced me, so I told them I'd have one drink. One drink, then I'm going home. Then I saw the most stunning girl on the planet the minute I walked in."

She'd given him a hard time about his pick-up line over the years, and it had become his way of showing affection, resurfacing throughout their relationship. It became their inside joke—and the cornier the better.

"I knew this would happen," he'd said two anniversaries ago as he stood in front of her with a bouquet of red roses.

"What?" she'd asked.

"That I'd buy a dozen roses and they wouldn't even compare to you."

She'd rolled her eyes at him playfully, but deep down she'd adored his sweetness.

Another night, they'd decided to walk home after a

decadent dinner at Vic's on the River. He'd come home that night with a bouquet of wildflowers—her favorite—and surprised her with the dinner reservations. As they strolled along the cobbled streets, he suddenly stopped as if he were frustrated.

"*I knew this would happen,*" he said before turning to Alicia, pulling out a ring box, and dropping to one knee. "*I knew when I saw you that night in the bar that I was in real trouble. Now look at me.*" He held up the ring. "*I'm absolutely, hopelessly in love with you.*"

Now as she surfaced from her bout of tears and self-pity —waves had hit her at random times since Bo's car accident nine months ago—she focused on the blurry figures on the television. Two anchors on the local news station were chatting, their desk draped in holiday greenery, their smiles painted on. Their mention of miracles just before the commercial break had gotten her attention. Probably because a miracle was the only thing that could save her now. She felt as if the walls of the condo were closing in, burying her alive.

A nurse by trade, Alicia's job in the orthopedics wing at Savannah General Hospital had saved her after Bo's death. Her education and training had taught her what she'd needed to comprehend that night: that the impact of the other vehicle, which had been traveling at high speeds when it hit Bo's car, had caused irreparable brain damage. Even if Bo had survived, his life never would have been the same.

Her work helped her escape the awful reality that followed. A natural nurturer, she threw herself into her job, taking extra shifts and staying late, even when she wasn't on the clock, just to avoid going back to the condo to be alone with her thoughts. She'd wanted to work through the holidays, but her supervisor, Katy Woodruff, insisted she take the time off through New Year's.

"But I'm the one who knows my patients," Alicia had countered. *"I give them every minute of my day. No one else will do that."*

"The patients need you to be rested," Katy said. *"You're exhausted. Look at you."* She waved toward a mirror in the break room.

Alicia had leaned in, viewing a face she barely recognized. Her long dark hair lacked the shine it used to have. She ran her fingernails along her scalp to her tight ponytail, straightening out the lumps. She had to admit she was thinner, the dark circles around her brown eyes accentuating the new angles of her face. Her skin was paler, the vibrancy that used to play in her features absent, as if she'd died with Bo and left her body behind to operate on autopilot.

"You're getting promoted in January, Alicia. You have to be ready to handle the responsibilities that come with that."

She needed this promotion. Bo's hospital stay and emergency surgeries, not to mention the funeral and burial costs, had racked up a ton. He didn't have life insurance, and the co-pays were thousands of dollars. Bo's family had tried to help, but they didn't have the money either.

She was barely paying the bills on her current salary, and this promotion would give her the security she needed after losing Bo's income. All their earlier discussions about her salary being only supplemental were out the window.

"I can't go back to my condo," she'd said to Katy, blinking away tears as she forced the words past the knot of grief in her chest.

Katy had put her arm around her. *"I hear you, but you can't keep going here either. You and I both know how easy it is to make mistakes when you're tired. I don't want you to push yourself until something awful happens.*" Katy gave her a squeeze before meeting her gaze. "*When was your last full night of sleep, hm?*"

Alicia hadn't had an answer because she didn't know.

Since work had been the only thing keeping her from crumbling, Alicia had gone home that day, fallen on the sofa, and cried herself to sleep.

She and Bo had chosen the condo in the heart of his hometown of Savannah, only about an hour from where she'd spent her late teens in Beaufort, South Carolina. After getting her nursing degree at Georgia Southern, she moved back home with her parents to save money. Bo had fallen in love with the exposed brick walls, high ceilings, and original ironwork still intact. Alicia was more impressed with the location and eager to fix it up and make it feel like home. Their plan had been for her to move in first and get settled, then when they were married he'd give up his apartment and move in with her.

When she wasn't working that first year she owned the condo, she'd spent all her free time nesting. She bought indulgently rich rugs to soften the cement floors, hung pleated white curtains with elegant tiebacks to feminize the wide 1920s windowpanes, and placed lamps and candles in all the quirky nooks and crannies. In summers past, her little kitchen table had held a bowl of lemons and glasses of sweet tea, and as the season changed to fall, platters of freshly baked brown sugar cookies. This Christmas it had held a stack of bills and a dirty plate from her take-out dinner for one.

"Deep in the wilderness of the Smoky Mountains"—the newscaster's voice sailed into her consciousness after the commercial break—"there's a covered bridge that many think is working miracles. Bridget Simpson reports live from the Noel bridge in the tiny village of Noel, Tennessee."

Alicia couldn't believe her ears. She'd lived in Noel until she was sixteen. She grabbed the remote and turned up the volume.

"Thank you, Tricia," Bridget said. She wore a bright red coat with fur around the hood, and her breath puffed out around her as if she stood in the middle of a blizzard. Stretching across the screen behind her was the familiar roof of the covered green bridge from her childhood with swags of snow-dotted holly and red berries around its entrance.

"This bridge might not look like much, but it's changing lives," Bridget continued. "Could Noel, Tennessee, an unincorporated community too small to qualify for a map dot, a village only notable for its proximity to the Great Smoky Mountains National Park, be the actual epicenter of Christmas? Decide for yourself."

Alicia spread Bo's blanket over her legs, transfixed as the television program clipped from person to person—each telling their story of how the bridge had changed their lives. One woman found her cat a state away from home after visiting the bridge. Another person had reunited with his cousin through nothing more than a wild coincidence when they'd both gotten lost while hiking through the area and ended up inside the bridge to find shelter from a storm. A couple had discovered the woman's misplaced family heirloom ring after visiting the bridge and wishing to find the lost item.

Once the spell of nostalgia had broken and another brightly colored commercial splashed across her television, Alicia blew out a cynical huff. They were giving that bridge too much credit. She knew all too well what the Noel bridge was capable of and what it wasn't. She'd spent sixteen years living near that bridge. The folklore had been so rooted in the small town's history that its magic was as real to the residents as the city council downtown.

The bridge had even granted Alicia a few requests as a child. She'd lost a tooth after hoping for it in the shade of the old clapboard structure. She'd won her elementary school science fair after a lengthy ask at the bridge, and she'd sworn her skinned knee from falling on the sidewalk in second grade had healed faster after she visited the bridge. But when she'd really needed it to deliver, when the outcome actually mattered, the bridge had failed miserably.

When she was sixteen and a half, she'd run into it, in tears after finding out her family was moving from Noel to Beaufort, South Carolina. Her dad, who'd worked outside his entire life, had gotten a job as a supervisor of a landscaping company in Beaufort, and the position nearly doubled his salary and allowed him to work at a desk for the first time in his life. He'd been thrilled, especially given his bad knees, but Alicia had not been. She'd rushed to the bridge and climbed the single step onto the wooden walking path lining the road that led inside the bridge and through to the other side. Out of breath, she'd pressed her back against the wooden structure and pushed her palms flat along the cool wall. She'd pleaded with whatever magic was working through that bridge that she'd be able to stay.

"I don't want to leave Noel," she'd sobbed, tears streaming down her face. "I want to live in Noel forever with the people I love."

When the sold sign appeared in her front yard, she hadn't wanted to believe that her request had gone unheard. The bridge's magic had always worked. Even without her smaller asks that had been granted, centuries of folklore around the structure proved that wishes made in the bridge came true.

She'd challenged her parents, not packing her belongings until the very last minute and, even then, deeming she was doing so for no good reason. The bridge would save her. She refused to believe they were leaving. Something big would happen to give her the house back. It had to.

Yet the movers had come and carried her boxes up the ramp of their truck until the house was empty. She'd left Noel feeling so betrayed that, even after college, she hadn't returned to her beloved town.

She'd told Bo the story and he'd grabbed her hands, pulling her off the sofa.

"We should go," he'd said, optimism filling his voice. *"It would be great. You could see all your old friends, show me where you grew up."* He leaned close and nibbled her neck, making her squeal.

She broke free and rubbed the goosebumps he'd caused on her arms. *"It's nothing special,"* she'd warned.

"You'll make it special," he'd said.

She laughed, shrugging off the compliment.

"I'm serious. It's good to get back to your roots." Bo grabbed her waist and pulled her back to him. *"And I'd love to see it."*

Sitting on her sofa in Savannah after hearing the personal desires that had come true for the people on the news program, she felt cheated. Why hadn't she received her miracle?

The news program returned and the next person they interviewed was a woman who'd lost her husband to cancer.

"I swear I could hear him speaking to me under that bridge."

Alicia sat up straighter and squinted at the television,

trying to sniff out anything in the woman's demeanor that suggested she was a fake. But the glisten in her eyes, the slight wobble of her lips—Alicia understood that so well—and the honesty in her gaze made it difficult to imagine this woman had any ulterior motives.

Could the bridge bring back someone from beyond? Could it piece together a broken life? Could it give her the future she'd lost? She rolled her eyes and folded her arms.

What Alicia understood most was the woman's *need* to hear the voice of her loved one again. For so many nights Alicia had strained to hear Bo's voice, pushing herself to the limits to conjure up the last time she'd been with him so she could decipher the rasp of his words or the light humor playing underneath them. She knew how easy it was to pray for it so hard that she could actually hear him. Perhaps the woman on her television had created her own miracle and opened herself up enough to remember the sound of her husband's voice. Alicia doubted the bridge had anything to do with it.

What might Bo say to her if he *could* speak? Would he impart some wise knowledge he'd learned on the other side, or would he simply say "hello" and let her move through life the way she'd been going? Was there some lesson she was supposed to learn from all this grief? Or was life simply unkind?

Given how the last year had gone, she was willing to bet on the latter. She couldn't help being a little angry with Bo, seeing how he'd left her before her life had really started and how he hadn't even been able to come back for her. Couldn't he have left her pennies from heaven or some-thing? If anyone could've done something like that, it would've been him. Bo had always been the guy who could make it happen, whatever "it" was. He somehow managed to get reservations at popular restaurants. When they were lost in a new city, he always found somewhere amazing to get lunch and had them back on the right path in less than an hour. Anytime she lost something, he was always able to find it. But maybe he didn't carry his life's talents with him when he died. That was how she rationalized his silence when she'd gotten too tired to be angry.

She clicked off the TV, folded Bo's blanket, and went into the kitchen to try to get herself together. She'd never climb out of her thoughts unless she cleared away the clutter in her life, starting with the kitchen table.

But as she cleaned up last night's dish, she couldn't get her mind off the bridge in Noel. The idea of a bridge granting people's requests and bringing them luck was completely ridiculous. How could a pile of wood with a roof have any magical powers at all? How could it bring about miracles? It certainly wasn't mentioned in the King James Bible she kept in the nightstand next to her bed. But she also remembered her mother telling her that God was capable of miracles, even today. Could He have some need to work through that bridge?

While Alicia carried on, absentmindedly tidying the living area and avoiding more tears, the past seemed to whisper to her, haunting her and filling her mind. It had been a long time since she'd been back home, since she'd stood under the bridge. Should she return to Noel?

The more she considered returning, with every pillow she straightened in her quiet condo, with each surface she wiped down, the less far-fetched traveling back to her remote little town sounded.

Christmas was in two weeks and she didn't even have a tree yet. She had no reason to decorate or celebrate the holiday. It might be nice to go back to Noel as an adult, see her old haunts... She was nearly certain the miracle of the bridge was all a hoax, but she didn't have anything else to do besides sit in the condo, missing Bo. Maybe the trip would be good for her.

Her parents had invited her to join them in Key West for the holidays, along with her older sister, Camille, and Camille's husband and their son, Oscar, but she'd declined, not wanting to put a damper on the trip and ruin the mood.

"You need to get out and let the sun shine on your face," her mother had said. *"There's something about the warm weather that recharges a person."*

Little did her mother know that Alicia's battery was beyond recharging. It was completely dead, like her dreams and her future. She'd tried several times to pick herself up and get out there again, but every time she'd been unable to do it.

"I worry about you—there all on your own," her mother had said in one final attempt to change her mind. *"Even if you don't go with us, get out of that condo. See something new."*

If Alicia went to Noel, she could, at the very least, convince her parents she was seizing the day and doing something for the holidays other than rotting in her condo in a haze of misery. She could tell them she planned to catch up with her childhood best friend, Evelyn Baton.

Growing up, she and Evelyn had planned to live side by side when they were older. But after she moved, they'd somewhat drifted apart—at least Alicia had. Evelyn still sent her messages through social media, but Alicia struggled to respond as often as she should have. They'd been so close as kids, and her parents would probably believe her if she told them she was going to visit Evelyn.

Getting away for a little while and going back to the

place where things had been so good might ease her burdened heart. After all, it was Christmas.

What she didn't want to admit to herself was her hope that being somewhere new might make her forget about the holiday entirely. Because if she let herself think about spending Christmas on her own, she might fall apart.

Chapter Two

Having caught the last flight out the next day, Alicia pressed her shoulder bag to her hip to fit down the narrow aisle of the plane without knocking into anyone. She passed a family, the two parents giggling over photos on one of their teenager's phones before the announcement to put the device in airplane mode. A few seats down, a father helped his young daughter get her seat belt clipped while she questioned him about the plane in rapid fire. A few people had already settled in, eyes closed, heads back.

Once Alicia found her spot, she inwardly squirmed when she had to ask an elderly woman, with a bag full of wrapped Christmas presents jammed under the seat in front of her, to get up so she could access the middle spot. A line of passengers formed behind Alicia as she waited for the woman to hoist herself up. When she finally succeeded, Alicia quickly took her seat and deposited her shoulder bag on the floor. She put her arm on the arm rest but then decided against it, wedged as she was between the old woman and a man by the window with his laptop open.

"The journey could be a little choppy, folks," the pilot said after they were in the air. "We'll be passing through a winter storm as we make our way into Georgia. Please keep those seat belts fastened."

The man beside her opened his laptop and connected to Wi-Fi, sending emails the minute they were told they could use their devices. Alicia wriggled her shoulders and tried to relax. But a tiny pulsing sensation had taken over above each of her eyes; she was parched, and having left her house at dinnertime, she hadn't really eaten, and the airport snacks of a cheese stick and packet of chips she'd downed on the way to the plane were fading quickly.

"Despite the weather, we're expecting a quick flight before we touch down in Atlanta. Enjoy the trip and happy holidays."

Alicia attempted to peer past the man's laptop perched on the tray to see through the window, but all she could make out was a solid blanket of velvety black, so she tipped her head against the seat and closed her tired eyes. Having caught the last flight out on a Monday night, the late time coupled with the altitude was doing a number on her head. As the plane cruised at 25,000 feet, she tuned in to the *shush* of the cabin air system and tried not to think about how easily she'd been able to leave her condo in Savannah.

There'd been no one in town to say goodbye to, no one at work to catch up on how to do her job while she was gone —Katy had already assigned her patients to another nurse— and there certainly wasn't anyone at home. Just for the sake of telling someone, she'd texted her parents and informed them she'd decided to go to Noel. Her mother had asked if she was going to stay with her old best friend. And Alicia had told her mom she was planning to see Evelyn, just to make the trip seem more normal. She hadn't actually planned to do anything special besides visit the bridge, and she hadn't called a single person to tell them she was coming—not even Evelyn. But she dared not disclose the foolish truth that she was going so she could speak to Bo. No one in their right mind would do something like that.

Alicia figured she'd let fate decide. If she was being ridiculous, maybe some cosmic force would stop her. Instead, she'd secured the last room at Fairlane House, one of only two bed-and-breakfasts just outside Noel. They'd had a last-minute vacancy. She couldn't believe it—especially during the holidays. She'd booked it right away, sinking more money into the two-night reservation than she really had available to spend. She'd never been to the bed-and-breakfast before and had no idea what amenities it offered. She hadn't bothered to view them because, truth be told, her options were limited. Besides, it didn't really matter anyway. She was only going for the bridge. She could sleep anywhere.

The flight attendants came down the aisle taking drink orders. Alicia declined and drifted off, trying to avoid her loneliness, if only for two hours and forty-five minutes.

The plane touched down in Knoxville, and Alicia quickly retrieved her rental car—a black Chevy Tahoe, an SUV bigger than anything she'd ever driven. The flight had been rocky due to the weather, but she was now an hour and six minutes into the hour-and-forty-minute drive through the Smoky Mountains of Tennessee. The SUV hugged the winding, icy roads while Alicia gripped the wheel tightly with both hands, feeling as if the vehicle straddled both lanes.

On this tiny road, she had no idea what she'd do if she met an oncoming car. Snow was bearing down with surprising force, piling up on the edge of her windshield, her wipers ineffective against the deluge. The radio went in and out, Christmas music fading to static noise then returning at unpredictable intervals. The rugged terrain required all her attention, so Alicia reached over and cut off the radio.

While on a brief straightaway, she turned up the heat, her low-country attire no match for the freezing temperatures a snowstorm could bring in this part of Tennessee. In her years away, she'd forgotten how cold it could be in the winters at this elevation. She'd thought she packed enough, but she hadn't planned properly at all for this amount of snow. And she definitely hadn't been prepared to drive in it. When she was sixteen, her father never allowed her to get behind the wheel in these conditions, and after they moved to Beaufort, there was barely ever ice on the roads, so this was a new experience entirely. Even with the yellow beams of her headlights cutting through the gray air, she could barely discern where the road actually was, apart from the steep slope up the mountain on one side and the extreme drop-off on the other.

By the time she finished the last forty minutes of the drive, her shoulders and back ached from the tension of her rigid posture. Her two suitcases slid across the back seat with the final turn, the sudden movement making her jumpy. Amid the haze of snow was the insignificant wooden sign that read *Welcome to Noel* in dark green letters. She slowed almost to a stop just after it and put her blinker on to turn left where the bridge stood about a mile down the road. She hesitated, staring straight ahead, indecision creeping in. What if she'd flown all this way and couldn't hear Bo? The reality settled in that he was gone, along with a certainty that she wouldn't hear him under some covered bridge in the middle of nowhere, and tears pricked her eyes. But then her mother's voice floated into her mind: *"God can work miracles anytime He wants to."*

Alicia had to commit if this little excursion was going to work. She couldn't go in with any doubt whatsoever. This was her only chance, and she had to give it everything she had—for Bo. Maybe he was waiting on the other side, eager to impart a few final words.

But after the late flight and treacherous drive, she was exhausted, and decided she should be better rested and prepared for the bridge and whatever awaited her there. Abruptly aware of the rumble in her stomach, she turned off her blinker and drove straight into town, hoping something was still open at eight thirty so she could grab a bite to eat.

The dark roads gave way to glittering holiday lights in the trees, and more strung between the two sides of Main Street, making Noel look like a wonderland in the snow. The wrought-iron streetlamps were adorned with bright red bows, and all the shops donned holiday wreaths and festive displays. A twinge of nostalgia took hold, and she remembered exactly why she'd wanted so badly to stay. She pushed the unanswered request out of her mind, not wanting to consider the potential ineffectiveness of the bridge's magic. Instead, she focused on how much her little town had changed in nine years. The old pharmacy was now a pet store, and the vacant storefront on the corner must have been bought by someone because it was now an ice cream shop.

The lone blinking sign at the end of the dark road grabbed her attention. The old diner had also been redone, and the "open" light was gleaming in the window. She pulled the SUV to a stop along the curb a few stores down. Using the rearview mirror, she wiped her fingers under her eyes to remove any wayward mascara and then fluffed her hair. She grabbed her handbag, opened the door, and hopped down to the frigid street. She tightened her coat in a poor attempt to keep out the cold as snow fell delicately.

Over the months since Bo had died, she'd built up a ritual anytime she was out on her own, for everyone else's benefit. She found out very quickly that if she went into a restaurant showing exactly how she was feeling inside as she ate alone, she got quite a few stares. One woman had sent a piece of cake over to her once with a message that said, *"I'm not sure what you're going through, but maybe this will help."* So Alicia had started walking in places with a forced smile, making small talk with the hostess, and then, once seated, she pulled a novel from her handbag and stared at it, pretending to be interested. Sometimes she actually read the book—on the days her grief would allow the printed words to reach her brain—but most of the time, she gazed at the ink on the page, her mind consumed with how different her life had ended up. She'd made sure to bring a book for this trip.

She worked up the polite smile she'd gotten so good at, squared her shoulders, and then stepped up to the diner's entrance. But just as she'd made it to the door, the open sign shut off, followed by the overhead light, plunging her into darkness.

She reached for the handle and pulled, but it was locked. One by one, the lights farther inside turned off. Her fabricated smile slid away. She stood there, trying to figure out where she'd get dinner now that the last place open in town seemed to be closed. She doubted very seriously Fairlane House would offer food by the time she arrived, since it was still a good thirty-minute drive out of town.

Then, she realized a dark figure was moving through the diner, heading toward her, catching her off guard. The figure was about Bo's size, his arms swinging slightly as he walked, just as Bo's had.

Every nerve in her body shot into action, her skin prickling with anticipation while the figure made its way toward her as if coming to see her specifically. Was she still asleep on the plane and this was some sort of dream? Or had Bo heard her pleading for him to come back before she'd even reached the bridge?

She forced her vision to fill in the gaps in his form through the darkness, nearly sure by his movements, that it was, in fact, her fiancé. She couldn't believe her eyes.

"Bo?" she whispered into the darkness, her heart aching to see him emerge through the door, that smile on his face as if he'd only been out of town these past months. *Please give me my miracle.*

Her heart slammed. She wiped the snow from her lashes, desperate to see him clearly.

When he got closer to the door, she blinked a few times as her heart caught up with her mind. The figure was someone else. Her breath caught as she tried to force the disappointment away and have one more second in that magical moment when she'd thought it was Bo.

The first thing she noticed as the man stepped into the light from the bulb that had popped back on above her were his blue eyes—definitely not Bo's hazel. He was also older than her fiancé—maybe thirty. His hair was dark brown, styled a bit shorter than Bo's, his jawline slightly stronger, and, upon closer inspection, his build was a little broader. Holding a box with the diner's logo, the man turned the lock and opened the door.

"Hey," he said, his attention flitting past her to the street. "We're closed."

The savory scent of whatever was in the box—a cheeseburger?—caused her stomach to rumble, but she barely felt it, her disillusionment overtaking the sensation. She nodded, unable to form words.

"Sorry. I was just here finishing some work, and I forgot to turn off the sign. We closed at eight."

His gaze had moved back to her, and she knew by the way his face softened that he could sense her grief and exhaustion. She tried to push the fake smile onto her lips.

"Okay," she said, attempting and failing to keep her voice even.

From memory, the closest grocery store was half an hour out of town—in a different direction to the bed-and-breakfast—her head was pounding, and her fiancé had just evaporated in front of her. It was everything she could do not to break down in front of this man.

"Come back tomorrow?" he asked, but what sounded like uncertainty saturated the question, making her look up at him. "You're not from here, are you?"

She shook her head. The complexity of the answer made her stammer when she started to explain, so she just trailed off. She didn't have it in her tonight to hold a regular conversation.

He cleared his throat and fixated on the street behind her, clearly distracted. Then with a small shake of his head, he turned his attention back to her.

"I'm Leo Whitaker." He held out his hand.

She shook it, noting his warm grasp. "Alicia Silver."

"You're freezing," he said, still clutching her hand. "I have a second if you want to come inside and warm up." He opened the door wider, allowing her entrance into the empty diner.

Had anyone else offered to take her into a dark, locked diner on a deserted street, she would have kicked him where it counted and dashed back to her car. But there was a gentle kindness in his suggestion, and she was just tired enough not to overthink it. She stepped inside, and Leo gestured to a table before turning on the lights over the hostess stand.

She took a seat. The salty scent from his box made her stomach growl again, loud enough to get his attention.

"The grill's off, but I made myself some dinner to take home." He came over to the table, set down the box, and pushed it toward her. "I'm not that hungry, so you're welcome to it."

"Oh, I couldn't," she lied through her teeth. She wouldn't admit that she could devour the entire box in less than a minute if she let herself.

"It's fine."

She shook her head. "I can't eat your dinner."

He peered out the window at the street once more and his shoulders fell. Then he held up a finger and went through the swinging double doors into the kitchen. Through the oval windows at the top of each door, the lights turned on then went back off. Leo returned to the table with two wrapped silverware bundles.

"We'll split it." He pulled out the chair across from her and sat. Then he unwrapped his silverware and opened the box, uncovering a pile of fries next to a toasted bun atop a fully loaded cheddar burger with lettuce, tomato, and onion peeking out the edges.

Alicia's mouth watered.

Leo stabbed the burger with his fork and dragged the knife through it. He slid one half and a few fries over to her side of the box.

"So if you're not from here, where are you from?"

She unrolled the paper napkin from her silverware. "I'm originally from here, but I moved away when I was sixteen. Now I live in Georgia."

He pursed his lips, appearing interested. How could she be interesting in the slightest? She was a shell of her former self.

"What about you? I don't remember you in school," Alicia said.

"I moved here from Chicago with my dad a little over a year ago. We wanted to relocate to a smaller town, and he asked to live in the mountains, so we searched online until we discovered Noel." His gaze shifted out the window and he looked at his watch, not saying anything more. He seemed to be in a rush.

They fell into silence.

Over the last few months, she'd gotten skilled at deciphering thoughts that lurked behind a pleasant expression. When Bo first passed, she searched the eyes of strangers walking by, hoping to see someone else who understood the storm raging within her. After a while, she'd settled into that storm, still taking the beating every single day, but no longer panicked by it. While she didn't look for it in others anymore, she could still spot the look occasionally.

Alicia picked up her burger and eyed the book peeking out of her handbag, feeling awkward sitting across from another person, neither of them evidently wanting to be there. Her head still pounded; she just wanted to eat in peace. She took a bite despite her perplexing company. The sharp cheddar and salty burger melted in her mouth, fueling her drained body. She hadn't tasted anything quite this good in a very long time. To her relief, Leo seemed just as pensive as she was, eating his half of the burger without a word.

When she stole a glance at him, he seemed preoccupied, there was an edge to his posture, as if he wanted to spring from his seat and run out of the diner. He hadn't taken his coat off either. At least he wasn't planning on staying for any length of time, which she was thankful for. Concerned that he needed to be somewhere other than there sitting with her, she ate as quickly as she could without giving herself a stomachache. It would be better to finish faster, anyway, so she could get to Fairlane House and check in.

When they'd both finished, their eyes met. He offered a little smile. While she tried to figure out his response, he got up and cleared their places, taking the container into the kitchen to throw it away. The upward curve of his lips lingered in her mind. It had been a long time since someone had looked at her like that.

She stood, pushed her chair under the table, and slid her handbag onto her shoulder. While she was still uncomfortable with other people, she was thankful she'd run into Leo tonight. Ten minutes later and she'd have been out of a meal. But her relief was for more than the food. He'd clearly needed to be somewhere else, yet he'd stayed. And he seemed okay with her silence, which made her feel slightly normal, if that were possible.

When he returned, he asked, "Where are you parked?"

She pointed toward the Tahoe. "Just down the street."

Leo led her to the door, let her walk out first, and locked up. "Mine's right in front of yours." He nodded to the Land Rover parked ahead of her rental.

As snow fell from the black sky, fluttering past the streetlamps lining the sidewalk, they walked toward the vehicles. She hadn't walked next to someone—together—in a long time.

"Thanks for dinner," she said just as they split to get into their vehicles.

"No problem."

Leo got into his SUV and shut the door. The engine started, the red taillights turning the snow on the hood of her vehicle crimson. Without allowing his engine to warm up, he pulled onto Main Street, heading toward a rural region, away from the residential area in town. Where was he going in such a hurry? She shook off the curiosity and started her SUV. She didn't need to fill her mind with anything else. She had enough to manage in her life.

As she made the thirty-minute drive out of town, the eerily dark, empty roads plunged Alicia into her inner self. That was the problem with being alone—she had nowhere to go but inside her own head. Which was a problem because there were no distractions to keep her from the one question that surfaced over and over: what had she ever done to deserve losing everything?

Her mother had taught her that everyone was put on earth for a purpose, and that purpose was woven into the fabric of their lives. Was she missing something in the big picture of her existence? Since Bo died, she'd been wandering aimlessly with no clue what was meant for her.

Bo would know. Was he actually there with her, and she wasn't alone at all? She sharpened her hearing, but the only sound was the quiet shush of her tires against the wet snow.

Wanting to believe in miracles, she contemplated what it would be like to hear Bo's voice again. She conjured the tingle that had spread down her limbs whenever he whispered in her ear and the strength in his arms when they had tightened around her in an embrace that always made her feel as if nothing could harm her. A lump formed in her throat and a tear escaped down her cheek. What good would hearing him do?

It didn't matter. Her selfish emotional side wanted to hear him, even though she knew the pain it would cause her. Maybe—just maybe—if he could get through to her, he could tell her what to do now.

Alicia was still wrestling with herself when she pulled up to Fairlane House and parked out front. She got out of the vehicle, pulled her suitcase from the back, then slipped and nearly fell as she hauled her bags up the steps.

Once she and her bags were safely on the front porch, she turned the doorknob, but it seemed to be frozen shut. She wiggled it again, but the door wouldn't budge. Putting her cold hands on her hips, she looked around for a doorbell, but there wasn't one, so she tried the knob again. Unable to get in, she knocked loudly, her frustration with the situation and her choices mounting. When no one came, she was nearly certain the bridge's miracle was that she'd freeze to death and finally get to see Bo in person on the other side. A part of her would welcome that.

Finally, the door opened, and Clyde Fairlane stood in front of her. "Well, hello!"

"Sorry, I couldn't get the door," she said, trying not to sound as flustered as she was.

With a grin, he pointed to the small sign next to the door frame that said, *Please use side door.*

Before she could respond, he threw a weathered hand to his plaid flannel-covered chest. "I wondered if it was actually you when I saw your name on the reservation." He grabbed her bags and pulled them inside. "How are your parents?"

"They're good," she said, stepping in.

He quickly closed the door behind her.

She remembered Mr. Fairlane from childhood. He'd been active in the town council and had enjoyed walking down Main Street, shaking people's hands and waving to passersby. His single mission was to get to know everyone in Noel because—and these were his words—*"If we all get to know each other, it's hard to get upset with an old friend. Our town will be better for it."*

"Sorry I got the wrong door." Alicia shivered in the lingering cold in the front entryway.

"It's no problem at all." Mr. Fairlane led her to the empty sitting room of the old Victorian house. A fire crackled in the fireplace under a mantle decorated with pine and holly.

"It's quiet," she noted, relieved.

"Ah, it isn't usually. In fact, it's been downright chaotic lately. We're booked solid because of the reports about the bridge."

Only then did she notice the fatigue that came with a busy day that had settled under his eyes.

"It's only quiet due to the late hour," he continued. "The guests have all gone up to their rooms."

Alicia was fine with quiet.

"Mildred's turned in for the night, but I'm gonna stay up for another hour or so in case anyone comes back down for a nightcap. Can I get ya anything? A cup of tea or coffee? Hot cocoa?"

"No, thank you. I'm exhausted from my flight, so I'll be the easiest guest ever tonight. All I need is a warm bed."

"Well, that I can certainly do." He flashed her a smile, his bushy gray eyebrows lifting. He picked up her bags, holding one in each hand. "Follow me upstairs, and I'll show you to your room."

The old steps creaked under Alicia as she planted each foot on the runner that led up the wooden staircase and followed Mr. Fairlane. At the top, they turned the corner of the narrow hallway before they stopped outside her room. Mr. Fairlane inserted a key into the lock, opened the door, and set her bags inside.

Alicia entered the cozy space. A fire was already going in the hearth across from a bed covered with a fluffy comforter and oversized pillows. A small Christmas tree twinkled in the corner.

"This is perfect. Thank you."

Mr. Fairlane handed her the key. "Mildred starts break-fast at seven, but I'm sure she'd like to say hello and catch up before that if you're awake. She's usually downstairs by six."

Alicia produced a smile for his benefit. "All right."

The man waggled a finger toward the fire. "You can use the wood stacked on the hearth. If you need any more, just call downstairs in the morning. The heat's pretty good, though, so if you get hot, just let it die down. We can start it for you again anytime."

"Okay."

"It's good to see you."

She smiled again, her eyes stinging from fatigue.

"Well, good night," said Mr. Fairlane.

"Good night."

When Mr. Fairlane shut the door, Alicia fell onto the soft bedding and closed her eyes. Her mind didn't have time to ruminate on anything else. She lost consciousness almost immediately, grateful for one of the few nights when sleep overtook her before her thoughts had time to consume her.

Chapter Three

Too early the next morning, Alicia stood in the hot steam of the shower and ran her hands over her soaking hair, the spray washing off the last twenty-four hours. What the water couldn't cleanse, however, were the blemishes on her battered soul.

While she'd fallen asleep right away, she'd awakened long before she was ready, another issue she'd been dealing with since Bo passed. Her racing mind would rouse her, but her eyes felt glued shut. This morning she'd rolled over to check her phone, only to find that it was 2:30. Her stomach had growled and she'd wanted to get up and make herself a cup of coffee, but she'd fought the urge. For the next few hours, she'd tossed and turned, trying to grab hold of any sleep she could manage.

Yesterday, she'd thought a night's sleep would make going to the bridge easier, but she'd been wrong. Her sadness was now followed by a paralyzing fear that hearing Bo speak to her would most certainly cause her grief to intensify.

She had the sinking feeling that returning to Noel had

been a terrible mistake. The only thing she could do in town was visit people from her past. Her old friend Evelyn would certainly be happy to see her—she was always messaging her on social media, asking her to come visit, chatting as if they'd never missed a day, and sending open invites to go skiing with her family, even though Alicia posted nothing online except the occasional restaurant check-in. She'd always told Evelyn she would find her the minute she got back to Noel, even though returning had been the last thing on her mind.

She scolded herself for not visiting Evelyn when she was a whole person before the accident. Or even in her younger days. But she'd been caught up in high school and then college. After that, she was busy finding a nursing job and working crazy hours because the young nurses were always left with the toughest schedules.

After everything she'd been through, the mere thought of having any kind of meaningful conversation was too difficult, so she'd decided not to let Evelyn or anyone else know she was in town. But even if she successfully avoided her old friends, she'd still have to catch up with Mildred since they were sleeping under the same roof.

Alicia rolled her head under the warm water one last time, then turned the faucet off, wrapped herself in a deliciously fluffy towel, and went into the room to get dressed. After slipping on an oversized sweater and leggings, she padded back into the bathroom to take a look at herself in the mirror. She hadn't done that often, but since she was going to be around people downstairs, she should probably look presentable. The more time she spent on herself, the less ragged she'd look, and the fewer questions Mildred would have.

She dug around in her makeup bag and applied foundation, spending extra time dabbing concealer on the dark circles under her eyes. Next, she powdered her skin and added a touch of blush, eye shadow, and eyeliner and a quick layer of mascara. With a swipe of lip gloss to finish the job, she looked a lot like she had before the accident, except for her thinner frame. She dried and curled her hair and viewed the final product. She'd managed to hide her brokenness almost entirely, which made her feel slightly stronger. If she could keep herself together on the outside, she might just fool everyone.

Downstairs, the dining area was quiet except for Mildred, who was in the corner arranging pitchers of coffee and mugs on a table full of gingerbread, buttermilk biscuits, and muffins set between poinsettias and sprigs of holly. The woman spread her arms wide when she saw Alicia.

"My goodness, child! You have certainly grown into yourself." She gave Alicia a big squeeze.

The feeling of someone else's touch was almost foreign.

"When you left Noel, you were all elbows and knees, just beginning to show your feminine side." She held out Alicia's arms. "Now you're a grown woman. And beautiful."

Alicia struggled to accept the praise. She didn't feel grown up *or* beautiful.

"How's your mom doing?"

"She's doing well. She and Dad are in the Florida Keys right now. Mom's avoiding the winter weather."

"Ah, I remember she didn't love the cold. She told me once that's why you all never had a dog. Your sister wanted one, but with her busy softball schedule, your mama knew she'd be the one walking the dog in the cold, and she couldn't bear it."

Alicia chuckled. "Camille is now a sports therapist."

"What a perfect job for your sister. She was also a football manager in high school, wasn't she?" Mildred offered Alicia the treats on the table.

"Yes, and she was on the gymnastics team. She'd compete in any sport they'd let her do." Alicia placed a piece of gingerbread on a small plate.

"Can I get you a coffee?"

"I'd love one. Thank you."

While she poured, Mildred told Alicia to choose a table and relax. Alicia took the gingerbread over to one of the handful of tables scattered around the room and dropped her handbag on the floor beside her. She dragged her fork through the moist bread and took a bite, savoring the warm, spicy sweetness.

"Cream and sugar?" Mildred asked from the coffee station.

"Yes, please. Heavy on the cream, if you would."

Mildred brought two mugs over to the table and sat across from Alicia. "What about you?" she asked before taking a sip of her drink. "What do you do now?"

The prickle of tension took hold, but Alicia grasped her mug to cover it. "I'm a nurse."

Mildred offered her a warm look. "I could see that. You don't have a negative bone in your body—always seeing the best in everything."

How times have changed.

"I bet you're so patient with people."

The direction of the conversation lightened Alicia's mood. The one ray of light she'd had these past months was the care of her patients. Being without her hospital family added to her struggles, and she couldn't help feeling bitter that Katy had sent her home for three whole weeks, until after the New Year. Now look at her—chasing a ridiculous idea that, if she were being honest with herself, she knew full well would produce nothing. Not to mention that she'd left the safe confines of her condo and forced herself out into the world.

The dining room was quiet. She'd expected it to be full of people when she came down. In the shower, she'd planned on there being a busy atmosphere to distract Mildred and make their reunion a little shorter. But with no one else there, the familiar pressure of needing to carry the conversation and interact settled upon her. She'd also hoped the other patrons' laughter and joy might drown out her feelings. For so many years, Bo had been the talker of their relationship, jumping into every conversation and making everyone laugh. She'd never had that kind of presence on her own, and without him in social situations, the silence was unbearable.

"I'm surprised breakfast isn't already busy," Alicia said.

"Oh, it will be, we're packed, especially now news of the bridge has gone national. Every room's occupied." Mildred squinted at the tray of biscuits, got up and positioned it a little closer to the muffins, then sat back down. "Right now, we've got a houseful of families. This place is brimming with kids. Which is why I made cookies at the crack of dawn." She winked at Alicia.

A spear of guilt jabbed Alicia in the stomach. Should she have spent time with her family instead of coming here? Should she have gone to the Keys with them? She knew the answer but didn't want to face it.

Her family hadn't been the same since they all moved to different states. Her parents were still in South Carolina, she was in Georgia, and Camille was in Maryland with her husband, William, and her son, Oscar. They didn't catch up the way they used to, and this trip would've given her time to be with all of them at once—an opportunity they didn't get very often.

"Besides, you're early," Mildred said, pulling Alicia from her thoughts. Mildred tipped her head toward the grandfather clock in the corner. "Breakfast doesn't start for another fifteen minutes. Then we'll have quite the crowd."

Alicia forced a smile.

"Well, young lady, what's on the agenda today?"

She'd come to Noel to visit the bridge. That was what she was supposed to be doing today. But she still couldn't bring herself to go. Just the idea of it caused the familiar lump of grief to form in her throat. She swallowed to ease it.

"Oh, maybe I'll just head into town."

"And do a little Christmas shopping?" Mildred asked, a sparkle in her eyes.

With her family in another state and all of them deciding it would be best not to swap presents this year due to the family's trip, Alicia didn't have a soul to buy a present for, but she nodded excitedly for Mildred's benefit.

"Want some actual breakfast before you go? I was about to put out the menus."

"That would be wonderful."

"Excellent. I'll go grab one for you." Mildred got up and walked out of the room, leaving her alone.

Alicia let out a breath and sat back in her chair, picking at the piece of gingerbread.

A few minutes after Mildred delivered the menu and returned to the kitchen, people began filtering into the dining area, taking seats at the other tables and sofas throughout the room, and chatting around the coffee station. Alicia rooted around in her handbag for her book, pulled it out and opened it, and began the task of looking occupied. What in the world was she going to do with her time? Maybe she should see Evelyn after all, find an out-of-the-way spot where they could catch up. She'd been okay one-on-one with Mildred, and she managed last night with Leo. Surely she could handle chatting with Evelyn.

Her mind went back to meeting Leo last night. That calm feeling washed over her again when the memory of him walking beside her on the way to their vehicles floated into her mind. Had he caused the feeling or was it being around people in general? The more she considered it, the more she was convinced he had an indescribable way about him that put her at ease. Perhaps his need to hurry had taken the pressure off her for once. And there was also the fact that Leo didn't know anything about her, so they'd stuck to surface conversation without getting into the weeds of her life story.

With one hand holding her book open, she picked up her mug with the other and took a long drink of the soothing, nutty coffee. She could always just take a walk downtown. Then she'd look as if she were window-shopping, but she wouldn't have to speak to anyone because she could act interested in something in a store window if anyone made eye contact. She could blend in with the crowd of strangers while she figured out what she wanted to do.

Yes, that was a perfect idea.

***

The snow-covered mountain town of Noel was stunning in the daylight. The old Main Street was flanked by preserved historic buildings, their storefronts pristinely painted, the original 1930s signs refurbished to look new. Every lamppost held a bright red banner with snowflakes and curly letters that spelled out *A Noel Christmas*.

A pinch of homesickness took hold, and Alicia's sixteen-year-old self bubbled to the surface. She tipped her head up toward the speaker playing Christmas music in front of the bookshop where she and Evelyn used to go after school and devour every paperback they could buy with their babysitting money. She peered past the twinkle lights and greenery lining the shop window, the rows of books in their polished oak shelves a blast from the past.

The memories of her time there made her want to cry for the young girl she'd been. If they'd never moved, where would she be now? Still hurting? Or completely happy? Could life have remained that simple forever?

She paused to view the pop-up ice-skating rink across the street. Red-and-white candy-cane-striped flags fluttered in the icy wind, alerting people that the rink was open for the holiday season. Bundled couples holding hands laughed together, wobbling and doubling over as they skated around the circle. Would she ever experience that kind of innocent joy again?

She paced along hilly Main Street. White lights glittered above her and in every tree that lined the busy sidewalk. Shoppers bustled by, holding steaming cups and shopping bags from the various boutiques. The town had certainly grown in the nine years she'd been away, and she was glad for it. This was a perfect place to blend in and disappear.

She continued walking, stepping aside for couples and groups every now and then as the sidewalk narrowed where small piles of snow hadn't been cleared. She peered into the shop windows, pretending to show interest in their wares, all the while wondering how long she could stand walking in the freezing cold. The smell of yesterday's storm, the feel of the icy pavement under her feet, and the rustle of the trees against the gray sky brought back happier memories of childhood, old friends, and the ache of leaving—or was it just the usual sting of grief with a Christmas-covered facade?

She stopped on the corner at the end of Main Street where the road forked and led out of town. Her childhood home was on a large plot of land, only about a two-mile walk down the left-hand lane. She dared not see it in her current state. That would do more harm than good, taking her out of the present and back to memories. Nothing remained of her years there anyway. Her high school bedroom was empty, and her swing on the old oak tree had been taken down—she remembered the day her father had removed it right before they left.

Perhaps she should go to the bridge and get the trip over with. Maybe she could even catch an earlier flight in the morning. She'd only planned to stay in town through tomorrow anyway, which was good since she didn't think she could stomach being there for Christmas. This had always been her favorite time of year growing up, but now it was too difficult, so she'd rather retreat to her condo.

Even though spending the holiday alone back in Savannah was bound to be depressing, her memories of Noel wouldn't be easy on her either. No matter where she was, she'd be miserable, and at least in her condo she hadn't put out any Christmas decorations to remind her of everyone else's joy. Maybe she should skip going to the bridge completely and go home before the next storm arrived.

She peered up at the white sign with curling blue lettering that read *Bridge Coffee and Tea*. Her hands were near frostbit; she could busy herself with grabbing a latte. The indulgence would be nice, and it would help keep her warm while she figured out what to do next. She opened the door and went inside.

As she made her way to the counter, the heady scents of caramel and cinnamon floated through the air, along with the smoky aroma of freshly ground coffee. Christmas music played through the shop, and a fire burned in the stone fireplace at one end of the seating area that was filled with plush chairs and pillows. With the snow piled on the window frame, the scene would've made the perfect postcard for the most discerning Christmas fan, but even with the atmosphere, all Alicia wanted was the warmth of a cup of coffee.

"Alicia Silver?" A shrill voice floated toward her.

Every hair on her body stood at attention, and blood rushed to her extremities as if she were a criminal, caught in the act. But in the act of what—living? She took in a steadying breath and turned to find a very memorable face. She'd know those green eyes and high cheekbones anywhere.

"Evelyn?" she asked, but she already knew it was her old best friend.

Evelyn rushed over and threw her arms around Alicia, nearly knocking her down. Then she pulled back and wrinkled her nose. "You were coming to surprise me and I spoiled it, didn't I?"

Well, Alicia had told her parents she was visiting Noel to see Evelyn, and this was definitely a shock... "Surprise," she said, pushing out a smile.

"I had no idea, I swear," Evelyn said, linking their arms as if they were no different now than they had been as girls.

Had nothing changed for Evelyn? Jealousy began to take hold, and Alicia pushed it away. Right after Bo's accident, that same feeling would wash over her anytime someone was happy. Their pleasure made her resentful she'd been dealt the hand she had. As time went on, she learned to ignore the feeling because she knew it would tear her apart if she let it.

Sometimes she wondered if she should tell more people what she was going through, but there never seemed to be a good time to mention grieving the death of a loved one. It didn't come up naturally in conversation, and if she brought it up, she was willing to bet whatever conversation had been going on would die in a hurry. So she'd stayed quiet. It was easier for her anyway.

"I was just coming in during my break to grab a decent cup of coffee before I head back to school," Evelyn said brightly as they took their places in the long line.

"School?"

Seeing her in the flesh took some getting used to. Alicia tried to reconcile the older version of her best friend with the little girl who used to hunt for four-leaf clovers with her in the backyard. Was her laughter the same as it had been? The sound of it echoed in her mind as she thought of them chasing each other through the large expanse of forest behind Alicia's house. Her parents had warned them not to go too far into the woods because they went on for miles. The girls had always followed the old hunting paths to be sure they could find their way back home.

"Yeah, remember?" Evelyn touched her shoulder, and Alicia scrambled to recall their conversation. "I teach at the middle school, but the kids are already off, and today's our last teacher workday, so as long as we get to school on time, we can pop out for coffee if we're quiet about it." Her eyebrows bobbed cheerfully. Then, as if suddenly attuned to Alicia's inner turmoil, those brows pulled together and empathy washed over her. "You okay?"

Alicia nodded. "Yeah, I just can't believe I forgot you were a teacher." But that was how grief worked—it clouded her brain like a dense fog at times, making her disregard the fact that the world continued to go on.

"Don't be sorry—you don't have to remember everything. It's been a long while since we've had a chance to catch up," Evelyn said, shuffling forward in the line. "Hey, what are your plans today?"

Alicia bit her lip. That was the second time she'd been asked that. Was this some sort of cosmic push for her to figure out what she needed to do? "I hadn't planned anything just yet."

"Well, I'm off at three," Evelyn said. "Why don't we meet at Deloris's Pie Shop for something warm and delicious? She still makes her salted caramel apple pie." Her friend stepped up to the counter and gave her coffee order.

Everyone in Noel knew about Deloris Colington's salted caramel apple pies. She'd been baking them every Christmas for decades. The crust was hand-made with dough shaped as holly leaves around the buttery, sugared edges, and the apples inside were coated in caramel with Deloris's secret collection of holiday spices. She only made the pies at Christmas, and each day she put a batch of ten out right at three o'clock after they were done cooling. She sold them by the slice or the pie.

When Alicia was growing up, they were so popular they'd sell out within the hour. Her mother had managed to secure an entire pie each year, and none of Alicia's friends knew how she'd managed to get them with such consistency.

The cheery nostalgia of the memory was enough to comfort even Alicia's aching heart. "That sounds amazing, actually," she said.

"Perfect," Evelyn said, showing a genuine happiness that Alicia hadn't been able to feel in nine months. "I'll meet you there. I'm excited to catch up!"

The barista called her name at the end of the counter.

"See you later." Evelyn left her to pick up her drink. Then she waved, slipped out the door, and left down the snowy street.

Alicia stepped up to the barista to order her coffee and couldn't help noticing how Evelyn had lifted her spirits. Her friend's warm smile and love for life had pulled Alicia out of her inner turmoil, and she was actually glad she'd run into her. Now, at least with a pie date on the agenda, she'd have something to do.

She found a comfortable nook at the back of the coffee shop with overstuffed chairs and low tables full of holiday magazines. She took a seat on the sofa and held her coffee in both hands, still attempting to warm up as the snow collected on the edges of the large window next to her. She decided to call her mother and report to her family that she was meeting Evelyn today, because they would undoubtedly ask when she spoke with them again. Since Bo's death, they'd been overly interested in her daily life. Her sister had her own family to manage, but she still called Alicia at least once a week, and her mother and father checked in almost every day.

She set down her coffee and pulled out her phone, then tapped her mom's name. "Hey," Alicia said when she answered.

"Hi!" Her mother's voice sounded a little too chipper, but it usually did. It was as if she thought she could produce enough happiness for them both.

"Are you in Florida yet?"

"Yes, we just arrived. There's a heat wave, and we're in

the upper seventies. My hair looks like a beehive with all the humidity, but the sunshine is glorious. I wish you were here."

"Honestly, I almost reconsidered," she said. She didn't admit that her reevaluation hadn't been based on what Florida could offer, but on what she faced here in town. "I just wanted to let you know I made it safely to Noel."

"I'm glad you called. I was planning to check in with you this afternoon. I heard about the snowstorm, and I was worried about you."

"It's still coming down," Alicia said, peering through the window at the snowflakes swirling in the wind.

"It's a relief to know you're safe. Those mountain roads can be treacherous."

"Yeah, I know. It was tough getting up the mountain in the dark." She picked up her coffee and took a long, soothing drink.

"They say more snow is heading your way, you know?"

Alicia squinted at the group of people bustling by outside. "I'm only staying today and flying out tomorrow."

"Well, you'll want to check your flight because it's supposed to get worse between now and the weekend. You should probably see if you can change your return trip and wait it out there until it's safer to get back to civilization."

Alicia didn't have enough money to stay any longer, so she changed the subject, figuring she'd most likely be able to fly back. It wasn't as if the airport couldn't de-ice a plane.

"There's more civilization here than there used to be," she said, her attention moving to the jingle of the bells on the coffee-shop door.

For the second time, a masculine frame caught her eye, making her do a double take. But on this occasion she knew it was Leo. She sank back into the sofa in the nook, to stay out of sight. From her vantage, she could still make out the side of his coat as he ordered. When she peeked around the partition, the barista's batting eyelashes and flirty grin aimed at Leo made Alicia concentrate on his features as he stepped to the side to wait for his order. In the light of day, his rugged good looks were more visible, and she understood why the barista found him attractive. But he also had a somber look, and he seemed to be in a hurry again, which was perfectly fine by Alicia.

"You-hoo..." Her mother's voice came floating back into her consciousness. "Can you hear me?"

She tore her eyes from Leo. "Sorry. I'm at a busy coffee shop. What were you saying?"

"In Noel? Well that answers my question. I asked how much it had grown. The words 'busy' and 'coffee shop' never would have come to mind when I think back to the little town we left."

"Lots of people have been coming to the bridge," she explained. "Apparently, news of the miracles went national. You know the drill."

A skeptical huff came down the line. "Only God can perform miracles."

"I know," she said, fighting the growing irritation at having wasted a lot of money coming back.

Her mother was silent on the other end of the line just long enough to give Alicia pause. She'd confided in her mom once about going to the bridge to ask for things when she was a girl, and how she'd believed it worked. Until the day they'd left.

"You didn't go back to get a miracle at the bridge, did you, sweetie?"

"Of course not," she lied through her teeth. "Why would I do that? It didn't work last time."

44

Her mom seemed satisfied with the answer, but it only made Alicia feel worse for even considering that the bridge had any magical qualities. She squeezed her fist, disappointed in herself for giving in to the old folklore.

Leo turned around with a cup of coffee and walked over to the cream-and-sugar station. Alicia willed herself to be invisible.

"How's Camille?" she asked her mom in a low voice.

"Good. You want to talk to her?"

"Sure." She was slowly slipping back into her low feelings, so she'd have to pretend everything was wonderful, which was exhausting. But staying on the phone would be a good idea since Leo probably wouldn't want to interrupt her if he saw her. She turned to the side and faced the wall, acting as if she were in deep conversation.

"Hello from paradise," Camille said.

"Hey, Cammy," she said, unconsciously slipping in her sister's nickname from when they were girls. Perhaps it was her mind's way of skipping over the trauma and focusing on better times.

"I can't believe you're in that freezing town when you could be drinking piña coladas in the sand with me."

It was good to hear her older sister's banter. She always dished it straight—it was Camille's form of affection.

"What's in Noel that could possibly be better than the Keys?"

Alicia didn't know. She'd given up a week of making memories with the living people in her life to stay with Bo, who'd never be coming back.

"It's the first time I've had built-in childcare since giving birth to Oscar," Camille continued. "Mom won't leave him alone, which is fine with me. I actually had time to get ready for the day. I'm not sure I've put on mascara in three years. I feel rested, like an actual woman and not just a lump of sweatpants. William will be all over me tonight."

Alicia grimaced, trying to get the picture of her brother-in-law seducing her sister out of her mind. "Eww, stop," she said, a laugh escaping despite her mood.

Camille laughed with her. "It's not too late to come, you know. You could be on a flight tomorrow morning."

She didn't know what to say. William was a pilot, and he was always flying them around. Alicia was willing to bet he could get her a ticket to Florida if she wanted one. There was truly no good reason not to go to the Keys. She just wasn't ready to feel jovial. It was as if that emotion had been ripped from her body and she couldn't get it back.

"Just think about it," her sister said into the silence.

"I will." Right then, even though she'd probably struggle to enjoy herself, she seriously considered jumping on the next plane anyway.

"Hey, I've gotta run. We're all waiting at a tiki bar, and our table's ready."

"All right. Have fun," Alicia said.

Just as she ended the call with her sister, Leo noticed her and held up a hand to say hello while he took a seat across the room. The tightness in his face revealed he had something on his mind, and while she was curious to know what it was, she knew better than to allow him into her world. She had enough problems.

She gave him a wave while checking her phone as if she had to be somewhere. Then she quickly stood, gathered her coffee and handbag, and headed out the door.

Chapter Four

Alicia jumped into the Tahoe, put it in drive, and maneuvered onto Main Street. It took until she was away from the center of the village before her wipers had cleared the snow from her windshield. She had no idea where she was going, but she couldn't stay downtown. Back home, she couldn't handle the solitude, but now she wanted to be alone. And if that meant she'd use up a tank of gas in the colossal machine she was driving just so she could have some quiet time, then that was what she'd do.

Camille was probably right. She should call her sister back and book the next flight out of there. She'd see Evelyn this afternoon and they could catch up. Then there was nothing more to do but leave. Right?

As she drove, the bridge kept whispering to her, calling her even though there was no point in seeing it. She could always go to the bridge after meeting Evelyn, and when the outcome was exactly what she knew it would be, she could go to sleep, get up, and fly to Key West to spend Christmas with her family.

Maybe it was a subconscious yearning or simply old routine, but when the rush of Main Street gave way to rolling hills of snowy farmland, Alicia found herself driving down the road where she used to live. She drove parallel to the barbed-wire fencing strung between wooden posts, which kept cattle in place on the Rockwoods' farm where she used to take horse-riding lessons every Wednesday with Camille. The fields were barren and covered with snow, the cows sheltering under the sheds at the edge of the property.

The pastures tapered off, the landscape changing again as the mountainous terrain took hold. A few cabins were still tucked away on the edges of the cliffs, their stone chimneys puffing smoke. Most of them had been rentals when she was in high school, so she didn't know if anyone lived there permanently now. She imagined a house full of vacationing family members playing card games and drinking hot chocolate while wearing fuzzy socks and lounging by the fire. Then the land flattened out a bit and there it was: her childhood home.

She slowed down to get a good look at it. The oak tree where her swing had been was standing strong, its limbs covered in ice. The windows of the clapboard bungalow were dark with no movement behind them, the driveway empty—no one seemed to be home. The side yard where she and Camille used to Hula-Hoop was hidden by snowfall, and the tree house her dad had built for them on the edge of the forest was no longer visible. It seemed to have been cleared away like everything else. The front porch had been updated, the old spindles replaced with more contemporary columns. The front door was new as well, the simple wreath of spruce complimenting the natural wood.

She stopped the SUV and zeroed in on the left dormer window in the arched roofline—her old room. What was it used for now? Did another little girl live there? Was it some-one's exercise room or home office?

As she pondered, her old life—her happy life—came rushing over her like a tidal wave, and tears pricked her eyes. If that little girl had known the heartbreak she'd endure as an adult... But no one could be prepared to lose the person they loved. It was unthinkable. But that loss *had* happened, and she was struggling to find her way to the other side. What if she never found her way out?

She wiped a tear from her cheek and tried to get herself together. Then she pressed the gas and drove away. Where she was going, she had no idea. As she drove, she felt more isolated than she had even back in her condo. While she'd wanted to be alone, she began to wonder if it wasn't really solitude she yearned for, but someone who could compre-hend what she was going through, and if she couldn't find anyone who understood, she'd rather be alone than try to exist in the regular world.

Her dreams and her future had died with Bo, and she didn't know how to live anymore. It was easy enough to tell herself to snap out of it, that nothing was going to change, and she had to learn to live with the loss, but she couldn't make her mind cooperate. Had she been irreparably changed? Would she never again fit in with everyone else?

A magnificently familiar sight came into view: the blue H hospital sign. Her work as a nurse had gotten her through the worst pain of losing Bo. Helping people was her way of giving back the one thing she really needed: care from someone who understood pain. And now, still struggling, she wanted to be in a place where she felt as normal as one could feel in her situation.

The next thing she knew, she was driving to St. Francis West Hospital. Maybe she could walk the hallways in the lobby for a while and pull herself together. She wouldn't have to carry on long conversations with anyone there, but she might be able to talk to other people who were hurting. Everyone else would be too busy to notice her at all.

She pulled into the front lot and parked the SUV in a visitor's spot next to a pile of shoveled snow. Then she got out and walked up to the entrance. The doors slid open and then closed behind her. The crisp atmosphere and smell of antibacterial agents and alcohol was oddly soothing. She went over to the visitor's desk draped with silver garland to check in.

"Who are you here to see?" the attendant asked. The woman's salt-and-pepper hair was pinned back with a Christmas-tree barrette, and a jingle bell hung from a red cord around her neck.

Alicia dug her hospital ID out of her handbag and showed it to the woman. "I'm just coming to observe," she said.

"All right. Is there a particular doctor you're visiting?"

"No, ma'am," she returned with a guarded curiosity. "I used to live here so I wanted to pop in." She gave the woman a reassuring smile, knowing there was no way she'd get upstairs without proper verification.

"You won't be able to leave the main corridor without clearance." The woman gave her a placating smile. "But you'll have access to the cafeteria, the lounge, and the hallway leading to the elevator. You'll need a code to board the elevator, though, and without a contact here, I'm afraid I can't offer you one."

"That's fine. The public areas will be great." Attempting to hide her disappointment, but understanding completely, she took the visitor sticker from the woman and placed it on her chest. Then, for good measure, she slid the lanyard with her nurse's identification around her neck.

As she walked away, the woman called to her. "Miss?"

Alicia returned to the desk.

"Would you like to volunteer? Here's the form." She handed Alicia the paperwork. "You could be volunteering by next week."

Alicia folded the paper and dropped it into her jacket pocket. "Thank you. I'll hold on to it for another time. I'm only going to be in Noel through tomorrow."

"Alicia Silver?" a voice cut through the conversation.

Alicia turned to see a woman walking toward her wearing scrubs. As the woman neared, Alicia recognized her old school friend Tabitha Brice. She was leaner than she had been growing up, making her features more pronounced. Her hair was the deep auburn it had always been and pulled back in a ponytail.

"It's been a long time, but you haven't changed a bit," Tabitha said, putting her hand on her hip, her diamond wedding set catching the light.

Alicia had nearly mastered hiding the little punches she received each day—couples holding hands, love songs playing on the radio, wedding rings to remind her of what she'd never have with Bo.

Tabitha moved away from the desk to allow a couple to get their visitor stickers, and Alicia followed. "Didn't you move to South Carolina?"

Alicia nodded. "I did, but now I live in Georgia."

"Oh, wow." Tabitha's unassuming pleasure was hard to match.

"You're a nurse," Alicia said, latching on to their shared profession. It seemed a fitting position for Tabitha. She'd been a caring person when they were growing up.

She used to stand up to the bullies at school when they set their sights on meeker kids. "Me too." Alicia held up her badge.

"I can't believe it. What are you doing at St. Francis West? Are you thinking of working here? We need people."

"I just stopped by. I was hoping to have a look around." She sent a glance of appreciation to the woman at the desk for trying to help.

Tabitha's laugh pulled her away from the desk clerk. "You're off the clock and frequenting a hospital? Why?"

Unwilling to delve into her story, Alicia shrugged and sent her phony smile across her face. "I needed to burn some time before I meet up with Evelyn and thought maybe I could take some ideas back to my team."

Tabitha lit up. "I should've guessed you two would be getting together. You were inseparable in school."

"I know." Getting back to her old life allowed her to escape the grief for a bit. She already felt lighter, knowing she'd see Evelyn again. She could rely on their shared experiences from childhood to fill the conversation, and with so little time before her flight out of Noel tomorrow afternoon, Alicia wouldn't have to worry about their chatting leading to Bo.

"Well, I work on the geriatric hall, and I'm on my break. But I can show you around up there."

"I'd love that."

Tabitha walked Alicia to the front desk attendant to vouch for her and get her a clearance sticker. Then they went over to the elevator, and Tabitha swiped her badge. The doors opened and they stepped in.

"So what brings you back to Noel?" Tabitha typed in a code, pressed floor two, and the doors shut.

"Oh, I thought it was time to pay everyone a visit. I

haven't been back since we moved," she replied with the best answer she could think of.

"The Fergusons will be happy to see you. Their offices are on my floor."

Dr. Mitchell Ferguson, Chief Executive Officer of the hospital, and his wife, Dr. Rose Ferguson, had headed up the hospital since Alicia was a child. Two of the most prominent Noel residents, their names were synonymous with St. Francis West, the largest employer in the area. The Fergusons were known throughout the community for their pro-bono work with veterans, and they supported all the town festivals with generous financial donations. Dr. Mitchell, as they called him, was known to do house calls in the middle of the night. He and his wife were also good friends with Alicia's parents—her mother had always called the Fergusons with any medical questions.

"I thought they would have retired by now," Alicia said.

Tabitha's eyebrows rose in what seemed to be agreement, but she said, "Still going strong."

"It would be just like them to keep working, even though they must be in their late eighties."

"Noel isn't really a magnet for medical professionals—who else is going to lead the hospital?"

Tabitha had a point. As long as Alicia could remember, the Fergusons had put everything they had into St. Francis West. They were the most trusted healthcare professionals in Noel. What would happen to the hospital when they finally did retire? Perhaps they'd asked themselves the same thing, which was why they were still there.

Tabitha nodded down the hallway. "Want to say hello?"

"I'd love to."

Alicia followed her friend past the nurse's station where, behind a small tinsel-draped tree with blinking lights, a few people sat on stools updating charts on their computers. One of them nodded hello to Tabitha when they walked by. Continuing down the hallway and maneuvering around a row of vital monitors and a folded wheelchair, they arrived at a door with a wilting holiday wreath. The door was cracked open, and the hushed voices coming from inside gave them both pause.

Tabitha peeked in through the crack, ready to knock, but then stopped. Blocking Alicia's view, she turned her head, placing her ear in the open space, her gaze moving around the hallway but clearly not taking in the view. A few seconds later, she stepped away, her eyes wide.

"Maybe another time," she said, grabbing Alicia's arm and guiding her to the other side of the door against the wall. "The sheriff's in there," she whispered. And then, as if something had registered, Tabitha's smile fell slack.

"What is it?" Alicia asked.

Tabitha grabbed her arm once more and whisked her past the nurse's station and back into the elevator.

"Where are we going?"

"Let's go to the cafeteria where we can talk."

Her curiosity getting the better of her, Alicia followed Tabitha through the main entrance to the other side of the hospital. They entered the empty cafeteria, and Alicia took a seat at one of the round tables while Tabitha went over to the large beverage refrigerator.

"Want a Coke or anything?" Tabitha called over.

"No, thank you."

Tabitha retrieved a bottle of soda and swiped it over the self-pay scanner, paying with her badge. When she returned, she opened the bottle and took a drink.

"What was that all about upstairs?"

Her friend looked around the empty room, then leaned toward her, despite the fact they were the only two there.

"So this elderly man who introduced himself as Dean came to us two weeks ago for tests for early stages of dementia," she said in a low voice. "He was adorable. He cracked little jokes that made no sense and he'd tickle himself." She laughed, clearly still affected by the memory of his humor.

But then her smile fell. "When we went in to take his vitals, the room was empty. Dr. Mitchell thought he had gone straight to the lab for bloodwork, and he went off to follow up. The rest of the day was so busy that I never had time to find out if Dr. Mitchell located him. But my friend Teri works in the lab, so when I saw her going home that day, I asked her if the old man had made her laugh, and she said he was bewildered when he got to her. They'd found him wandering the halls a floor down." She took another drink, then twisted the cap back on, fear in her eyes. "He was discharged that same day, but I wondered if he should have been."

"I just heard the sheriff in the Fergusons' office, and he said the man has been missing since Sunday. They've been making the rounds everywhere he might have gone in town, and they were checking to see if anyone had brought him here."

The anxiety that had plagued Alicia since Bo's passing welled up with ease. "Oh, my goodness. That's terrible." She recalled how cold she'd felt walking in town earlier. "I hope he's inside somewhere."

Tabitha nodded. "Me too. And with the storm expected to worsen tonight, there's no way he could survive out there." After a pause, hope filled her expression. "Given how witty he was with me and how 'with it' he seemed to be at times, I'll bet he's gotten himself somewhere safe and just hasn't been able to let anyone know." The glisten in her eyes betrayed her lingering distress.

Alicia's chest tightened. "What does he look like?"

"Thin, thick gray hair, long face..."

"No striking characteristics I could be on the lookout for?"

Tabitha shook her head. "Not that I saw."

Alicia pulled out her phone. "What's your number? I'll send you mine. Could you let me know if you find him?"

"Of course."

———

Alicia's trip to the hospital hadn't been quite as soothing as she'd thought it would be, and she was relieved to park in front of Deloris's Pie Shop to meet Evelyn. She scanned the passersby as she walked around her SUV and stepped up on the sidewalk, pausing to look around for an old man who appeared lost, but nothing seemed out of the ordinary. She tugged on the large wooden door and let herself into the cozy space.

One of the original buildings on Main Street, the pie shop occupied the old pharmacy that was originally built in the 1950s. The pie shop was on the bottom floor and Deloris's apartment was upstairs. The long soda fountain counter was still in place, the stools re-covered in a soft blue to match the updated interior. Along the surface of the counter sat every flavor of pie imaginable, cooling on rattan mats.

"Well, butter my backside and call me a biscuit, if it isn't Alicia Silver!" Deloris tossed a pair of floral oven mitts onto the back table and swished around to Alicia's side of the counter. "How's your mama'n them?"

"Good," Alicia replied as Deloris wrapped her in a warm hug. The sight of the woman pulled her right back to her childhood, when she and Camille used to sit on those stools and spin around as they waited for a slice of pie. She was glad for the distraction from the worrying news she'd heard at the hospital about the missing man.

"Glad to hear it. They here?"

"No, they're in Key West. I'm the only one who opted for snowstorms this year."

Deloris bounced with a jolly laugh. "Well, I'll warm ya right up. Whatcha fancy?"

"The salted caramel apple pie, of course. Is there any other option this time of year?"

Deloris wrinkled her nose playfully. "Y'all got here just in time. I've got two slices left." She turned toward the back wall. "Evelyn, you want one too?"

"Yes ma'am!" Evelyn waved to Alicia from one of the rows of rocking chairs.

Deloris went around to the other side of the counter. "How about a scoop of vanilla ice cream to go with it, like you used to ask for when you were girls?"

"I'd love that." Alicia went over to her friend and took a seat beside her.

Evelyn scooted her teacher bag out of Alicia's way, allowing more foot room. "You been keeping busy today?"

"Surprisingly, yes."

Evelyn rocked in her chair. "It's so good to see you."

Deloris walked over, carrying two plates of steaming pie, and leaned toward the window. "It's really coming down now. I hope y'all can get home okay." She handed a plate to each of them. "Where you stayin'?"

"Fairlane House." Alicia set the plate in her lap, careful

to keep it steady so the already melting ice cream didn't drip over the edge.

"Lucky girl." Deloris brightened. "How long you stayin'?"

"I'm only here through tomorrow."

Evelyn leaned forward, her face aghast. "What? That's not long enough to catch up."

"It was just a quick trip."

"Well, I'm honored you'd come into my shop when you're here such a short time."

"Too short," Evelyn added. "I thought we'd have more than just today."

Alicia struggled to keep the guilt from rising at the sight of concern in her friend's eyes. If only Evelyn knew what it had taken to get her here.

"What time is your flight tomorrow?" Evelyn asked.

"Eleven o'clock."

"Promise you'll at least meet me for breakfast before you leave Noel?"

"I need to get to the airport an hour before the flight, I have to return the rental car, and I'm flying out of Knoxville. It's an hour and forty-minute drive."

Evelyn's expression fell, but she tried to smooth it out while dragging her fork through her pie. "It sounds like you're coming up with reasons not to have breakfast."

Called out, Alicia's cheeks burned. "It isn't that I don't want to…"

"You were my best friend for almost sixteen years," Evelyn said. "I finally get to see you again, but it's so rushed. Is there something important you have to get home for?"

The question hung between them, and Alicia struggled for an answer. There was literally nothing calling her back to Savannah.

"I'm going to run to the bridge and ask for you to stay," Evelyn said with a playful twinkle in her eye.

Alicia forced a smile.

Her friend nodded toward Alicia's plate. "You haven't touched your pie. It's Christmas," she said, waving a hand in the air. "Even if I only get a short time with you, let's make it great." She scooped up a forkful of flaky crust piled with caramel filling and popped it into her mouth.

Alicia did the same. It took only one bite of the gooey center and crisp tartness of the apples to remind her of all the good things she'd left behind.

"I'm hoping having great conversation with me will convince you to stay so I don't actually have to go to the bridge," Evelyn said, winking. "Since we both know that bridge doesn't do a thing."

Alicia had to fight the idea that her friend was right.

Chapter Five

By the end of their pie date, Evelyn had convinced Alicia to meet her for breakfast the next morning at Bridge Coffee and Tea. And the truth was, she didn't mind. For the last hour, the women had reminisced, chatting about their childhood—how they'd spent hours reading in the top bunk in Evelyn's bedroom, devouring book after book, and how they used to get off the school bus together and race Camille to the front steps of Alicia's house. While they'd chatted, relief had taken over Alicia. It was easy to spend time in the past, before Bo, when her world had been happier. Remembering those things made her realize how much of her life had been wonderful.

"I get up before the sun most days," Evelyn said as they stood on the snowy sidewalk before parting ways and heading to their cars. "Wanna meet at seven? Would that give you enough time?"

"I think so," Alicia replied. "I'll call you if I'm ready before then." She was actually hoping to get there early. She wanted to spend more time with Evelyn. Revisiting her old life had made her feel unbroken for a while.

Evelyn reached out and gave Alicia a hug. "See ya tomorrow!" As she paced down the sidewalk, she called over her shoulder, "My next challenge is to convince you to change your flight." She giggled and ducked behind a parked car before crossing the street during a lull in the oncoming traffic. With a wave, she disappeared behind the holiday crowds.

Smiling despite herself, Alicia climbed into the Tahoe and started the engine. She blew on her cold hands and rubbed them together, waiting for the heat to warm them up. It was nearly dinnertime, and she was hungry. She could stop by the diner for a bite to eat, but instead she drove the other way, out of town, toward the bridge.

Even though Evelyn had repeated what Alicia already thought about the bridge not having any real power, she drove there anyway. She knew exactly why. Real miracle maker or not, the bridge was the reason she'd come to Noel. With breakfast in the morning and a flight out after, this was her last chance to go. Tapping into the Alicia of her youth, she felt strong, but she knew her strength probably wouldn't last, so if she was going to go, she had to do it now.

By the time the green clapboard of the old bridge came into view, she'd mustered all her courage. She came to a stop at the end of the line of cars driving slowly through it, their taillights bright against the darkening sky. She pulled out of the line of cars and turned down a side road to park along the curb. She jumped out and, sliding the keys into her pocket, paced across the grass, the snow already past her ankles.

The cold wound its way down into her shoes, giving her a shiver, but she kept going. Stepping onto the narrow pedestrian walking path paralleling the road and leading through the bridge, she was plunged into darkness. The only illumination was from the beams of headlights of car after car. She stopped midway to allow her eyes to adjust and leaned against the wall, her heart pounding. She could run out and back to the security of her vehicle, but she forced herself to stay.

She closed her eyes and tipped her head back, preparing to send her thoughts to the heavens. With a deep breath, she let the words go: *Bo, are you here?*

She tried to sift through the echoey shushing of the tires on the road, imploring Bo to respond to her. She'd been a good person. She worked a job of service helping others. There was no reason she shouldn't get her miracle when all those other people had.

Bo... I just want one last chance to talk to you...

She strained to hear anything at all.

But as she said the words again in her mind, a tug in her heart pushed her to wish for something else, surprising her. She wrestled with whether her time with Evelyn had somehow prompted it. The more she considered what she was about to ask, the more she realized that the thought was right.

Bo, she sent into the air. *Or God—whoever can hear me up there... I have something new to ask. I'd like...* She swallowed, trying to get the words out. The silence that surrounded her caused her to open her eyes, and she realized the last of the cars had gone through. She was the only one inside the bridge at that moment. She struggled to see in the pitch-black darkness without the beams from the cars.

Mustering all her courage, her final thought formed and lifted into the heavens: *I'd like to be able to feel whole again.* Like a helium balloon, her words floated away silently on the air as tears brimmed in her eyes. How nice it would be not to carry the incredible weight of grief.

A sob rose in her chest as if it had been held down for all this time and only now was released. She suppressed it to maintain the silence as she pleaded with Bo to promise he'd help her. She was so tired. The last nine months had all but emptied her, and talking with Evelyn had made her wonder if there was more life for her—if she could just get through this. She kept her eyes closed and stepped into the center of the path, sharpening her hearing, knowing the bridge had no power, but holding out hope all the same.

A soft voice drifted toward her in a whisper: "I knew this would happen."

Alicia gasped as she stood in the pitch-black of the bridge, trying to decide if she'd really heard what she thought she had. That line had been their inside joke—no one could've known it.

Bo?

Suddenly she realized that maybe Bo was teasing her for wanting to move on. Her hands trembling by her sides, she widened her eyes in the darkness to try to see him as the sound of shoes moved toward her. Every nerve in her body was on high alert. Would she get to touch him? Would this be her miracle?

Whack! She was on her back on the wooden walkway, someone pretzeled on top of her. Did Bo have a different scent in the afterlife? She grabbed his bicep, trying to right herself.

A voice that wasn't Bo's hit her like a smack in the face. "I'm so sorry."

A familiarity whirled through her, but she struggled to place it without all her senses present. While she was still trying to digest whose voice it was, a blinding white cell phone light shined into her face. She let go of the man's arm and shielded her eyes.

"Alicia?" A hand took hers and helped her up. The man moved the light to his face. It was Leo. "I'm so sorry. I didn't know anyone else was in the bridge. It was so dark..." He turned the light toward the walkway. "Are you all right?"

"Yes," she said, still breathlessly trying to make sense of what had happened. "What were you doing inside the bridge?"

He let out a tight sigh. "It's a long story. Where's your car?"

His brisk redirection was a tactic she'd often used, and she stared at his shadow, wondering what he might be there hoping for. She pointed to the side street just as a few cars drove past, illuminating the snowy route.

"Want to follow me back into town?" he asked, his words laden with an undecipherable heaviness. "I feel terrible for knocking into you. Since dinnertime seems to be our thing, and I'm starving, we could get something to eat."

She hesitated, unsure what was holding her back. It could be a nice distraction from her thoughts about Bo. She could've sworn she heard him just before Leo knocked into her. "Sure."

They stopped at the Tahoe.

"I'm just there." He pointed down the street. "I'll meet you at the diner."

"Okay." She got into her vehicle and started the engine while watching Leo walk away in the rearview mirror. She let out a loud breath as if she'd been holding it in and rested her forehead on the steering wheel.

It wasn't Bo, she told herself. *You didn't hear him. The bridge doesn't have any magical qualities whatsoever. It was Leo.* But why would he say the exact words Bo would've probably used in that moment? She squeezed her eyes shut and tried to remember the precise sound of the voice. Had it been Bo after all? It was low and almost inaudible and there was no way to know. She wanted so badly to believe it had been her fiancé, but her rational side wrestled with her hope. The niggling feeling deep down, however, was that if it *had* been Bo, maybe he'd heard her asking him to help her move on with her life.

She put the car in drive and swung the massive SUV around in the middle of the snow-filled street, heading for town. The whole way there, her mind was a muddle of everything she'd been through that day. From her hospital visit to meeting Evelyn to the bridge just now, she'd been on a roller coaster of emotions. It was incredible how much she'd endured in a single day. She'd lived more life in one day in Noel than she'd lived in months back home.

She pulled up at the diner the same time as Leo, and they got out of their vehicles and met at the door. Through the window, the place was humming, the dining area lit brightly and full of patrons. Leo opened the door for her then followed her inside. He waved to the hostess, grabbed a menu from the stand on the wall, and then led Alicia to one of the few empty tables at the back of the dining area. He pulled out her chair and she took a seat.

"Funny that we'd run into each other two nights in a row," he said, handing her a menu.

"Yeah..." she said, still trying to make sense of everything.

A waitress came over and took their drink orders, and while Leo exchanged a few pleasantries with her, those whispered words came back to Alicia once more: *"I knew this would happen."* She racked her brain for context. If it had somehow been Bo, what would he know? That she'd be a wreck without him? That she'd put her faith in some ridiculous legend?

The waitress left, and she forced herself back into the present.

"So why were you at the bridge?" she asked Leo again.

He put his elbows on the table and clasped his hands. "It's all my fault," he said, his thoughts clearly elsewhere.

"What's your fault?"

His chest filled with air, and he turned his attention to Alicia. "My dad's missing. I went to the bridge hoping for a miracle."

"Missing?"

That thing she'd seen in his eyes earlier had made it to the surface. "He has early-onset dementia. He's an outdoorsman, and I think he wandered off for a walk to find a good place to relax for the day because his walking boots are gone, along with a blanket and his fishing gear, but I fear he got lost right before the snowstorm blew through."

"Yesterday?"

He shook his head. "He left Sunday before the first round of snow. And now it's getting worse." Worry lines creased his forehead. "Everyone's been looking for him for the last two days. We've checked all the riverbanks and streams, the forest at large, but so far there's been no sign of him."

"Is his name Dean?" she asked.

Leo lit up, hope in his eyes. "Yes. Have you seen him?"

She shook her head. "No, but I heard the sheriff was looking for him when I was at the hospital today."

"You were at the hospital?"

"Yeah," she said. "I'm a nurse and I stopped by to... see a friend."

The waitress returned with two sodas and set them down along with a couple of straws. They ordered food and then fell back into their conversation.

"I'm sorry about your dad," Alicia said, her heart breaking for him.

He chewed on his lip and his jaw clenched. "Thank you. It makes no sense. He has moments of confusion, but he's never shown an instance of being unaware of his surroundings. He might forget why he went on a walk, but he'd know if he was getting too cold. I've been looking everywhere."

Now it all made sense. The night she met Leo, he wasn't late for something. He was worried about his father out in the cold. He was looking at his watch because he was anxious about the late hour and his father being out in the snow somewhere. If she'd known, she would've insisted on going out to look for him with Leo.

"We moved from Chicago to Noel to try to keep him safer after he began showing symptoms of dementia. He lived with me in Chicago and would sit in my small apartment while I worked all day, which is no life, *and* I knew that with his condition worsening, our quality time together would be limited." His eyes glistened. "I still remember the day I walked into the living room and set a US atlas on the coffee table. He looked at it and asked what it was for, and I told him it was our future. Then I asked where he wanted to live. He put me off at first, saying we couldn't move. When I pushed him about why, he gave me a look and said because of my job. I had worked my way up to become executive chef at Claude Audoux's, one of the most prestigious restaurants in Chicago. Dad said he was proud of me and didn't understand why I'd want to move.

"My mom died when I was a teenager, and we promised her we'd always do what made us happy. I reminded Dad of that promise and confessed that I wasn't completely happy with life in Chicago. I told him I thought

I'd be happier in a small town where we could spread out instead of being confined to a tiny high-rise. And that I'd been thinking about opening my own restaurant.

"That got his attention. He seemed excited about the possibility, and the diner was really his idea," Leo continued. "Dad loved to cook, too, and opening a diner had been his dream as a young man, but he'd given it up when I came along, instead sticking with his more secure job at the post office. I wanted to see him live out his passion before it was too late."

Leo had put his father above himself, something Alicia could relate to, given her career in nursing, and she couldn't deny how much his gesture warmed her heart.

"But I got so busy running the diner that sometimes I had to leave him home by himself, and we were in the same boat again." He blew out a breath and peered across the dining area and out the window. "I keep hoping he'll show up here..."

He pointed to a booth near the door by the hostess stand. "He likes to hang out there and read his novels. Every day the table is empty, I feel like I can't get a full breath. We've looked for him everywhere, but there are so many deep valleys and high mountains around here. It's impossible to comb through it all. Especially in the snow." His eyes shimmered, his lips set in a pout. "We're losing too much time, and he's frail. I don't know how he could survive for two days in this."

"My friend is a nurse at St. Francis West. She talked to your dad when he was in for bloodwork."

Leo met her gaze.

"She thinks that given how witty he is, he's probably gotten himself somewhere warm and just hasn't been able to let anyone know."

Leo nodded, although he didn't seem convinced. He looked again toward the window. The snow was coming down as if someone in the heavens was dumping it by the bucketful.

With a deep sigh, he turned back to her. "So why were *you* at the bridge?"

She fiddled with the straw paper on the table in front of her. "My fiancé died nine months ago," she said, surprising herself. She couldn't remember the last time she'd said those words aloud. "I wanted... to be able to cope, to move on, because I feel like I'm in quicksand."

She stared at the table for several seconds. When she finally lifted her gaze and made eye contact with Leo, his taut jaw had softened, his expression conveying interest.

"I'm sorry," he said softly.

"It's okay," she replied, using her standard response. It was an odd reply, given that nothing was really okay, but it seemed to set people at ease.

Leo's pout took shape again. "When my mom died of leukemia, I had to learn how to live with a gaping hole in my life. It wasn't okay," he said, as if he'd read her mind. "It still isn't. I miss her every day. After a while, that hole became a part of who I am, and I learned how to carry it with me."

"Do you ever wonder where she is now?"

"All the time." He breathed deeply and then exhaled. "My dad missing rips right through me and takes me back to losing my mom. I can't lose him too."

Alicia felt the prick of tears.

"Christmas is my dad's favorite time of year. So if I have to lose him, it can't be now."

The clatter of the diner faded away, and in that moment it was just the two of them. Someone else who knew her kind of grief.

Chapter Six

The next morning when her alarm went off, Alicia rolled onto her back and tried to gain focus through the gray light filtering in through the window of her room. After everything that happened the day before, she'd been as exhausted as she was when she had long shifts at work, and she'd fallen right to sleep. And, surprisingly, she hadn't stirred in the night once.

As she lay there in the light of day, Leo's missing father was the first thing that came to her mind. Was he out there struggling somewhere while she'd been cocooned in her soft bedding? The image gave her a shiver.

The fire Mr. Fairlane had started for her last night had been reduced to glowing embers. All she wanted to do was throw another log on it and curl back up under her fluffy blankets and close her eyes. But her mind was too busy, she had a flight to catch, and she'd promised to meet Evelyn for breakfast.

She climbed out of bed and started the shower, testing the water until it was warm enough to get in. After a deep breath, she leaned into the spray to let it run over her face.

Eyes closed, her mind plunged into the memory of standing inside the bridge in the darkness, that all-too-familiar phrase filling her mind: *I knew this would happen.*

It had only been nine months, but already she couldn't be sure if it had been Bo's voice she'd heard. How could she not be sure? Was she already forgetting what he sounded like?

She didn't want to think about it, so she put her focus on washing quickly, drying off, and getting ready for the day.

With her suitcases packed and the room tidied, she lugged her bags down the stairs, then opened the app on her phone to check in for her flight. The app wouldn't load. With a sigh, she swiped it closed and then reopened it.

Mrs. Fairlane came around the corner. "Checking out with no breakfast?"

"I'm meeting Evelyn Baton at the coffee shop."

"Oh, that's wonderful. I'll bet the two of you have some catching up to do."

"Yes," Alicia said to be agreeable.

"I hope you can get out," Mildred said. Before Alicia could respond, the woman was already moving away from her. "Stay right there. I'll get Clyde. I'm sure he'll want to see you off."

Alicia wasn't sure she had time to wait, but she did want to see Mr. Fairlane. It would be nice to tell him goodbye. She tried again to get the app to open, but it wouldn't.

"You'll have to connect to our Wi-Fi or I doubt you'll get service," Clyde said, coming down the hallway. He pointed to the sign with the log-in and password.

"Why's that?" Alicia put the phone into her back pocket.

Mr. Fairlane tugged open the front door and an arctic blast took her breath away. She gaped at the thick blanket of white covering everything, including her Tahoe. Only a haphazard path about a foot wide had been shoveled out to the road.

And the snow continued to fall.

Her first fear wasn't how she'd get to breakfast or if she'd make her flight. She thought of Leo's dad. No one could survive outside in all of this. She wanted to check on Leo to see if he was okay and if there was any news about his father.

"We've had blizzard conditions over the last two hours. The plow's gone through on the main roads, so you can probably get into town, but my parking lot is still a block of ice and snow. I called a snow removal company, but they're backlogged, as you can imagine."

"How long until they can get here?" she asked while switching her phone over to Wi-Fi and logging in to her airline's app.

"They said three hours at the least."

Her shoulders fell. "I'm going to miss my flight."

Mr. Fairlane closed the door. "On the news this morning, they said the storm was pretty wide. There are considerable delays and cancellations. It's worth checking to see if your flight is still scheduled."

With a sigh, she rubbed the cold off her arms. "Well, is there any way I can tack on another night or two here?"

Indecision spread across his face. "I'm sorry. The room is booked and the couple is already here."

"How?" she asked, more to herself than as a question for Mr. Fairlane.

"Their friends somehow managed to drop them off this morning. I have no idea how. They're waiting by the fire in the lounge until the room is ready. It's their anniversary."

"They couldn't stay with their friends for a few nights,

since it's an emergency?" She felt terrible even asking, given that they were celebrating.

"I'm not sure." His gaze moved back and forth as he considered. "You could stay on the sofa in our suite."

"Thank you. That's very kind," she said.

She didn't want to put them out *or* sleep on their sofa, but what other option did she have? She needed to call Evelyn and let her know she was snowed in and then try to call the airline. And she needed to alert the rental company that she wouldn't be able to return the Tahoe today.

Alicia patted her suitcases. "Do you mind if I leave these here and make a few phone calls?"

"Not at all. Come, come." He beckoned her. "Sit by the fire. Would you like a mug of cocoa or anything?"

"No, thank you. I'll be fine."

"All right. Let us know what you decide."

"Okay."

The couple taking her room was deep in conversation, laughing over a half-empty carafe of mimosas. Alicia went over to one of the chairs in the corner by the Christmas tree. She searched for the airline's number and called them first. As expected, the line was busy, so she tried the car rental company's number from her confirmation email. No luck there either. With only ten minutes until she was supposed to meet Evelyn, she called her friend.

"Hey, I'm sort of... stuck," she said when Evelyn answered. She explained the situation quietly so as not to disturb the happy couple across the room.

"Don't worry," Evelyn replied. "My car's been in the garage under my apartment in town all night, and the garage opens to the main road. Everything between here and the Fairlanes' has been plowed. I can be there to get you in about five minutes."

"Okay," Alicia said.

"See if you can make it out to the main road."

Alicia ended the call and slumped back into the chair. She should've gone to Key West with her family. What was she supposed to do now?

She took in a slow breath and let it out, trying to clear her mind. She'd had harder days than this, and she knew what she had to do: take things one step at a time. She'd focus on getting to breakfast. Once she was in town, she could try the airline again and hopefully still get a flight out today.

She buttoned up her coat and tightened the belt. Then she found the Fairlanes to tell them she was going into town and she'd let them know if she couldn't get a flight. With resolve, she took a suitcase in each hand and went out into the frigid air to make her way up to the road.

It wasn't long before Evelyn's Honda appeared. Her friend stopped in front of her and popped the trunk. Alicia put her suitcases in and shut it. Then she climbed into the car, relishing the warmth.

"Can you believe all this?" Evelyn asked as she turned the car around in the middle of the empty street. "We haven't seen snow like this in ages."

"It's unbelievable. I've got a rental vehicle I'm paying for by the day, and if I can't get to my flight, which may already be canceled, I'll have to sleep on Clyde and Mildred Fairlane's sofa. They've already booked my room for tonight."

"You can stay with me. I'm off for Christmas break except for the Christmas production, and I need to spend" —she threw up air quotes—"*quality time* with my parents and make our annual gingerbread house. It usually takes us a couple days, but otherwise, with all this snow, I'll be bored stiff. We can bake Christmas cookies, drink too much wine, and binge on late-night movies."

The offer was definitely more enticing than her alternative accommodations.

"It'll be fun! Like old times." Evelyn made the turn to head toward downtown.

Alicia tried to decide which option would be more exhausting. Spending time with Evelyn had been easier than she'd expected. And it was bound to be a few days before she could get out.

"It's really not an imposition, if that's what you're worried about," Evelyn said. "I have a two-bedroom apartment, so you'd have your own room."

Her own room... "All right," Alicia said. "I'll just have to let the Fairlanes know."

Evelyn squealed in excitement.

Was she really up for this? Alicia wondered. Since losing Bo, she hadn't spent a full twenty-four hours being social with anyone.

Evelyn pulled into an open spot near the coffee shop and they got out of the car. Despite the snow, the shop was still busy. The small chalkboard sign outside boasted, *The warmest spot in town!* with little holly leaves drawn around it.

Alicia immediately thought of Dean again. There was something tragic about the situation that had settled in her gut and wouldn't leave her alone.

"Hey, do you mind if I run down to the diner really quick? I want to talk to Leo."

"The owner?"

"Yeah."

"Well, you're in luck." Evelyn pointed through the window. Leo was inside the coffee shop, standing in line.

An unusual sensation washed over Alicia this time—relief. While she'd spoken to countless people at work and in the days after Bo's passing, she couldn't deny the difference between those experiences and the one she'd had yesterday with Leo when he'd told her he'd lost his mom.

Evelyn reached around her, opened the door, and they went inside. "I'll get us a table and breakfast menus."

"Okay," Alicia replied, already focused on Leo. "Be right back." She crossed the busy shop and tapped him on the shoulder.

Leo turned and then stepped out of line to greet her. Her pulse raced with worry at the sight of the dark circles under his eyes.

"Hey, I was about to run over to the diner to check on you. Any news on your dad?"

He shook his head, his lips turned down in anguish. "I've been up all night looking for him. I drove the streets until it was too dangerous to drive." Tears welled in his bloodshot eyes, and he cleared his throat. "The sheriff's office has been combing the woods. Dad was in the military... He can survive this, right?"

Leo's question didn't have a helpful answer. The reality was that Dean was an older man battling dementia, and it seemed impossible for anyone to survive exposed to the elements they'd had recently. But Alicia spoke the same unwritten language as Leo: the language of grief. Leo was in the moment just before it all came crashing down and his world changed forever.

She remembered that space in time vividly. She'd been in that state in the hospital when she'd gotten the call that Bo had been in an accident and was clinging to life. She recognized all too well the sour mixture of hope and agony that soaked through every ounce of Leo's body. This was the wait before the irrevocable answer that could change his life forever.

She put her hand on his arm and gave him an affectionate squeeze to soothe him. To her surprise, he pulled her in for a hug. As her face lay on his chest, the scent of cotton and cedar filling her nose, she realized he needed her to help brace his emotions. The feelings were so big it took both of them to manage them. The same spirit of helping others that had drawn her to nursing gave her strength now. She shouldn't have any left, given how she'd handled her own grief, but with Leo, she felt strong.

"I knew this would happen," he whispered.

Her breath caught and she understood that the whisper she'd heard at the bridge had been his. Until that second, the phrase had been locked away in her memory, but now it was tangible, as if it had its own form and floated in the air between them.

He let go of her and looked into her eyes. "I can't get it out of my head. I *knew* it would happen."

She had to force the words out. "How could you know?"

"The day I left him at home, something told me not to. But he seemed fine, and I had a ton of work. Getting the staff fully trained and the business side of things up and running was so much... I worked later than I should have, and the whole day I kept feeling that I should go home. But I'd reassure myself that I'd left Dad food in the fridge and he'd just be sitting in his chair reading when I got there."

"You couldn't have known."

"Excuse me," the barista cut through their conversation. "Are you ready to order?"

Alicia looked around. The line had disappeared, the last person now waiting for their coffee. As Leo stepped up to put in his order, Alicia spotted Evelyn waving from a table across the room. She leaned toward Leo.

"I'm here with a friend, but I'll catch up with you."

"All right."

"Don't leave without coming over." She pointed to Evelyn's table.

"Okay."

Alicia moved across the room toward her friend.

"Wow, you move fast," Evelyn said with a wink as she approached.

The statement was jarring after her conversation with Leo, and she struggled to make sense of it. "What?"

Evelyn nodded toward Leo. "You're only here a couple days and you're hugging the most eligible man in Noel. I like your style." Her eyebrows bounced.

"Oh," she said, gathering what Evelyn must have witnessed. "It isn't what it looks like." She didn't want to get into it right then, so she left it at that, but Evelyn clearly wasn't convinced. Alicia picked up her menu and focused on the choices, finding a few that sounded great. "Why don't we go order while the line is down?"

They got up and went to the counter to order their breakfast. Leo was already at the other end, waiting for his coffee.

"Introduce me," Evelyn whispered.

Given Leo's state, Alicia felt the need to protect him. "I told him to come see us before he left. I'll introduce you then."

"Good idea." Evelyn nodded. "That way it looks less contrived." She grabbed Alicia's arm and pulled her close. "You know, every single woman in town is itching to get to know him."

"Really?"

"Yes. But he doesn't give anyone the time of day. We started to wonder if he was already taken, even though we've never seen anyone on his arm." She turned and gave the barista her order, then motioned for Alicia to do the same.

"I'll have an oat milk latte and the egg and bacon croissant, please," Alicia said.

Leo took his coffee to one of the chairs by the fire and pulled a book out of his coat pocket. When he opened it, she couldn't help but wonder if he was actually reading it. Surely she was the only person who pretended to read in public places.

"I can't believe you're on hugging terms already," Evelyn continued once the barista had rung them up. She handed the woman her credit card and the woman handed her their table number. "You must be able to work miracles."

"Believe me when I say I *cannot* work miracles."

Evelyn shrugged off her coat and draped it over her arm. "It appears that you can."

They made their way to the end of the bar and when their coffees were ready, they took them to their table.

Alicia slid her coat off, hung it on the back of the chair, and sat down. "I'm not sure he's in the mood for socializing."

Evelyn glanced over at him. "Why?"

"His dad's missing."

Her friend's eyes rounded. "I'd heard that the other day. No one's found him? I'd assumed they had."

"No." Alicia fiddled with the lid of her coffee.

"That's terrible."

Her friend turned toward the door and stared silently. Alicia imagined she was thinking if Dean was out there, there was no way he'd survive.

"I wish I could help him," Alicia said.

Evelyn took the lid off her coffee and blew on the steaming drink. "If anyone can, it seems that it's you."

"Why would you say that?"

"Well, don't make it obvious, but out of the corner of my eye I can see him, and he keeps looking over at you."

While Alicia had originally wanted to stay clear of people, Leo was different. She felt a connection with him, an unspoken bond, and she couldn't let him sit there if he needed her for any reason.

She got up. "Call me if the food comes. I'll go see if he needs anything."

Evelyn's face was written with uncertainty, but Alicia walked over to where Leo was sitting. He closed his book and set it in his lap.

"You're welcome to sit with us if you want to," Alicia said. "My friend is overly chatty and maddeningly positive, but she means well."

He leaned around her and surveyed their table. Evelyn offered an unsteady wave.

"I'll have to pass today," he said, offering her a small twitch of a smile.

"I get it," she said. "Let me give you my number. I'd like to know when they find your dad."

He pulled out his phone and she gave him the digits, then her phone pinged in her back pocket.

"I just texted you so you'll have my number too. Check in any time you want."

"Okay."

Evelyn beckoned her over as their food arrived. When Alicia turned to walk back to their table, her feet were frozen in place. Every fiber of her being wanted to go back to Leo and help him find his dad.

Chapter Seven

L eo hadn't stayed at the coffee shop long, and Alicia had eaten her breakfast about as quickly. Now she was lugging her bags up the indoor staircase to Evelyn's apartment.

"I hope the kids can make it to dress rehearsal tomorrow," Evelyn said as she took one of Alicia's suitcases.

Alicia shook her sore arm, thankful for the help. "When is dress rehearsal?"

"Nine in the morning." Her friend hoisted the luggage onto the next step. "It doesn't look like this snow will be going anywhere." She stopped at the landing and leaned on the window ledge. "Temperatures aren't supposed to get above freezing all week." She pushed away from the view and started up the stairs once more.

The thought gave Alicia a shiver. She was unsettled knowing Leo's father was out there.

"It's the last rehearsal before the show Friday night," Evelyn continued, but Alicia barely heard her friend, her mind still on Dean.

They arrived at Evelyn's apartment and she slid the key

into the lock, opening the door and allowing Alicia to enter. As expected, the space was cozy and filled with Christmas décor. They set Alicia's bags on the living room hearth under the striped stockings and swags of greenery and surveyed the twinkling Christmas lights on the tree in the corner.

"I'm pretty sure the kids will get there if they can, though," Evelyn said, as if talking herself into a positive outcome. "These are the kids who would rather do a play over their Christmas break than stay at home. They're great kids." She set her keys on the small bar separating the kitchen from the living room and dropped her purse on one of the stools.

"I hope they all make it," Alicia said absentmindedly.

"Have a seat." Evelyn offered the sofa and Alicia complied. Her friend dropped down next to her. "You're still thinking about Leo's dad, aren't you?"

Alicia's shoulders relaxed in surrender. "Yeah. I wish I knew where to look. I'd go out there myself and try to find him."

"You and I both know the woods around town like the backs of our hands, but it wouldn't be safe to go out in this weather. The last thing we need is three people stranded in the elements. We'd freeze ourselves."

"I wonder what he was thinking, the fear he must have had when he couldn't find his way back." A lump formed in her throat and she attempted to swallow it. "We should go look for him anyway."

"I heard he went missing from his home. Is that right?" Evelyn asked.

"I think so."

"We don't know where that is. As far as I'm aware, Leo doesn't live in town. And depending on how far out he lives, you and I probably aren't any better off in the wilderness than his father. You know how those steep valleys can come out of nowhere."

"I feel so helpless. He deserves to have all the people who can be out looking for him."

"I know how you like to save the world—it's the trait that makes you an incredible nurse, I'm sure—but you can't save everyone."

Truer words could not have been said. If Evelyn only knew that she hadn't saved Bo and she'd barely been able to save herself.

Suddenly, she was aware of Evelyn's hand on her knee.

"Something has changed in you. What is it?"

"What do you mean?"

"I know you're worried about Leo's father, but there's something else... That fire you used to have isn't quite as strong as it was. It's as if something has beat you down."

It would only be a matter of time before she'd have to explain her life, and since they'd be living under the same roof until the snow melted, she better tell her friend sooner rather than later.

"I was engaged to be married..." she began.

Evelyn was supportive and thoughtful, listening to Alicia's explanation of the last nine months. When Alicia finished, it felt like a bit of the burden had been lifted. She'd told Leo and now Evelyn, and she'd made it through both times without completely falling apart.

"I'm glad you came back to Noel this Christmas," Evelyn said.

"Me too." And she actually meant it. "I haven't felt much like celebrating until I came here."

Evelyn's somber face lifted. "You feel like celebrating?"

"It feels more like Christmas now that I'm with an old

friend." For the first time in a very long time, she felt the draw of looking ahead. In Noel, life felt more normal, as if she'd left the old her behind in Savannah and here, she'd found the girl she used to be.

Evelyn stood. "Let's get you unpacked and comfortable. *Then* we can really get you into the Christmas spirit." She lifted one of the suitcases. "I say we turn on holiday movies, bake cookies, and drink wine all day and into the night until we fall asleep."

"All right. I just need to see if I can change my flight."

"Make it for next week," Evelyn said, her eyebrows bobbing up and down happily.

Feeling a little lighter, Alicia followed her into the guest room.

"I'm wondering if we should switch to coffee—maybe decaf, though, since we've passed the two o'clock hour," Alicia said through the slight haze of alcohol from her third glass of wine.

The airline had been busy, so she'd given up trying to change her flight and settled in for the rest of the day with Evelyn. They'd been drinking wine while baking cookies and doing laundry, which she had to admit was a helpful diversion.

"I'll make us some." Evelyn whirled around and opened a canister of coffee, the strong, almost chocolatey aroma filling Alicia's senses.

Alicia surveyed the kitchen. Both the counter in front of her and her clothes were covered in flour. The scent of apples and sugar lingered in the air, and the kitchen was warm from the cookies in the oven and the rows of them cooling on the counter. A Christmas movie on the living room TV hummed in the background, although she and Evelyn had spent so much time chitchatting that neither had paid any attention to it.

Conversation came surprisingly easily now that she had nothing to hide. She'd been able to relax into the day-to-day conversations two people who hadn't seen each other in years would have. They reminisced about their childhood, and Evelyn had reminded her about their nature walks through the woods, way farther than her parents allowed, searching for pine cones. They would cover each scale of the cones with peanut butter and then sprinkle birdseed on top before hanging them from trees so the blue jays could have food.

At times Alicia sensed the conversation moving toward Dean and the mood shifted, but they seemed to have a mutual understanding that worrying about Leo's father would always be present.

That shared understanding was what Alicia had been missing of late. For the last two hours, she'd felt almost normal. The razor's edge she'd been teetering on since she lost Bo had faded away. Was this the next step in the healing process? It made her wonder if the bridge was magic after all. But then, Dean hadn't been found safe.

"While you make the coffee, I'll try again to get through to the airline," Alicia said.

"Why don't you see if they have a flight after the weekend? You could go to the middle-school play on Friday. The kids have done a remarkable job. They built and painted all the scenery. It's incredible. It's only about an hour and a half long and starts at five. We could get drinks after or something. I'll be busy directing, but it's going to be really cute. We're doing *A Christmas Carol.*"

Maybe it was the wine or the glistening snow outside the window, but Alicia liked the sound of going to a Christmas play. Especially for a story about how generosity and compassion reformed a cold heart. She took in the pleading look of her friend.

"That sounds great."

Chapter Eight

Alicia finally got ahold of the airline the next morning. Her original flight had been canceled, so she'd been able to change it to the following Friday. She also extended her rental agreement for the Tahoe. Being in Noel had shifted her focus, given her a different side of life to consider, and while she'd eventually have to face her life in Savannah without Bo, she wanted a little more time to avoid it.

So she'd decided to stay through to next Friday and get home just in time for the weekend before she had to go back to work that Monday. Doing so put her in Noel for Christmas, and she wasn't sure where she'd be staying or how she'd handle it if Dean hadn't shown up on his doorstep by Christmas Day.

At the moment, with Evelyn at rehearsals and at least a couple of hours to kill until she returned, Alicia sat alone in the apartment and nibbled on one of the gingerbread cookies they'd made the day before. She clicked on the TV and flipped through the channels, but nothing caught her eye. She stood and walked over to the window. The street below had piles of plowed snow on each side, the pavement beneath like a black stripe against the snow-covered ground. The apartment was just high enough to make out the wave of the tree line along the mountains. It would be a beautiful sight if she wasn't worried Dean Whitaker was out in it. She went back over to the sofa and decided to text Leo to check in.

> Any news?

Right away, she got a response.

> Nothing. What are you up to?

She texted that she was at Evelyn's while her friend was at rehearsals for the school's play for the next two hours or so and she was going stir crazy.

Leo texted back:

> I had another sleepless night and I'm in need of food and someone to keep me from falling asleep. Think you'd be up to the task?

She couldn't ease his burden, but she could definitely be a sounding board. And his company would be nice. She replied that she'd meet him at Bridge Coffee and Tea in fifteen minutes. Then she wrote a note telling Evelyn where she was off to and pocketed the spare key her friend had left for her. She put on her coat and scarf before heading out the door.

Alicia crossed her arms to keep warm as she walked down Main Street toward town. It occurred to her how easily she'd been able to open up to both Leo and Evelyn. It was as if her past and present were colliding. Evelyn had been a connection to a happier time of her life, and she'd initially connected with Leo because they both knew about loss, but she also felt an element of hope when she was with him.

When she arrived at the coffee shop, Leo was waiting outside. He held up a gloved hand to say hello. She was clearheaded enough today to notice how handsome he really was, even though it was clear he was tired and under a lot of stress. She could see what the draw was with the ladies in town. When her eyes met his, something deeper than his surface charm seemed to connect her to him.

He held the door open for her and they went inside. Once they ordered, they took a seat at a table near the fireplace. The flickering embers warmed her.

"So what's the latest from the sheriff's office?" she asked, jumping right in.

Leo rubbed his eyes. "They've got nothing. They've been combing the woods, but haven't had any trace of him, and the new snow has covered anything that might have given them a clue."

"And you're sure he hasn't somehow managed to travel somewhere to visit anyone?"

"We don't know anyone close by and no one has reported finding an old man." A look of exhaustion washed over him. "It's been too long... I'm starting to consider this a recovery operation and him no longer a missing person." He was having a difficult time keeping himself together. "How many days do I go before I stop looking?" The last word caught with his emotion, and he cleared his throat. "I feel like I'll never stop."

Alicia chewed her lip, shaking her head. "I wish I could do something. I want to help."

A small smile formed on his lips. "You are helping."

The waitress brought their plates of food. Alicia had opted for brunch, ordering the frittata and French toast, while Leo chose a sandwich.

"How am I helping?" she asked once the waitress had gone.

"You're the first person I've actually gotten to know a little bit since I've been here. And it's easy to talk to you. When you arrived that night on the doorstep of the diner, I was about to crack under the pressure of it all. But you softened the blow."

Completely consumed by her own grief at the time, she hadn't considered that she was helping anyone. And yet somehow she had. But he'd made her feel better as well.

"You did the same for me."

His cheeks flushed and he offered her a wide smile, the sight taking her breath away. Then he tucked in to his breakfast, still pensive. His red eyes turned down to his meal.

"You need to sleep," she suggested.

He took a sip of his coffee. "I can't. The minute the search teams stop for the night, I'm out searching. The nights are the hardest." He shook his head. "I don't know why I keep going out after sundown. It's too dark to find anyone. But my alternative is to sit in the house and do nothing."

While knowing Bo's fate had crushed her, Alicia couldn't imagine the paralyzing feeling of *not* knowing.

"I've had a lot of volunteers helping," he said. "They tell me to give myself a break, but what will I do? What would take my mind off it?"

"They're right, you know. You'll do no one any good running yourself into the ground." An idea occurred to her.

"This is a long shot, but would you like to go with me to my friend's middle-school play tomorrow evening? She said it's only an hour and a half long, and it might give you a mental break."

"I've got a couple of employees who can handle the weekend crowd at the diner... Yeah. I'd like to go," he said, to her complete surprise.

"I hope it's okay, but I invited Leo to the play tomorrow," Alicia said when Evelyn arrived home.

Her friend lumped her coat on the edge of the sofa and dropped down next to her. "Of course it's okay to bring eye candy to the play!"

Alicia laughed. "Seriously, I think it might help lift his spirits."

"Yeah, good thinking." She kicked off her shoes and folded her legs underneath her. "Do you know anything about him?"

"Not much, to be honest. We just sort of connected."

"Well, it's rumored he had a long-term girlfriend before he moved here, but his dad's care sort of put a damper on things and they broke up."

"I lost contact with people after Bo's death. Life's trials can put a strain on relationships that aren't built on a strong foundation. But I'd never imagine losing someone I was close to."

"Maybe they weren't as close as he thought," Evelyn said. She pulled the throw pillow from behind her and set it in her lap. "When he first got here, he was the talk of the town: eligible bachelor, newly single, independently wealthy... Remember Sheila Jacobson?"

"The prom queen?"

"Mm-hmm. She asked him out, and he turned her down."

Alicia sucked in a breath of surprise. Sheila Jacobson wasn't used to hearing "no" back in high school. "How did she take it?"

"She hasn't been fluffing around town since."

"Oh, my."

"Yet you're getting hugs *and* he's agreed to go to a school play with you. How are you doing it?"

"Doing what?"

"Swooning him? Have you been to the bridge?"

The question surprised Alicia, pulling her from the moment. "Why?"

"I wondered if you wished for a handsome suitor or something."

Their collision that night floated into her mind. "We both know the bridge doesn't have any powers whatsoever."

Right?

"Yeah, you're right," Evelyn said. "I wished for something to happen with Andy Nelson and it never did."

Alicia folded her legs under her. "Oh, I forgot you had a crush on him."

"I still do," Evelyn said, her cheeks growing rosy. "I think he might feel the same, but we just can't get our timing right." She put her feet on the coffee table, crossing her legs at the ankle. "I have to admit that I wished for him inside the bridge."

"And nothing happened?" Alicia asked.

"Nothing yet!"

The thing Alicia loved most about Evelyn was her optimism.

"I'm leaning toward a seven-letter word," Evelyn said as she set letter tiles on the board of the old game of Scrabble that was spread out between them on the coffee table that evening.

"Don't tell me that," Alicia said with a laugh as she picked up her glass of wine.

"Why not? You wouldn't actually let me win, would you? You always manage to win."

Alicia rearranged her letters. "How do you even still have this game?" she asked before building on a word in front of her.

"I have all the games we used to play." Evelyn drew her tiles and pumped her fist.

Though unwilling to spend too much mental time back in Savannah, Alicia couldn't think of a single board game in her condo. Where had they all gone? Bo hadn't enjoyed board games. He was always on the move, gravitating to social activities and traveling. Even when he came over to their condo, they spent their time having long conversations and philosophical debates. But there was a nostalgia to doing this that centered her. She imagined what it would be like to play with her children one day. If she ever got the chance.

"Okay, I think I have an eight letter word—alfalfas," Evelyn said before taking a proud sip from her wine glass.

With a smirk, Alicia shook her head. "Can that be plural?"

"Definitely. I win. Unbelievable."

"We used to keep track of all our wins, remember?" Alicia asked.

"Yes, I do. I probably have the list tucked away in one of

the other game boxes." The oven beeped and Evelyn got up off the floor. "Pizza's ready."

Alicia took her wine and followed Evelyn into the kitchen. "We used to play board games all winter long when we couldn't be outside. I loved it."

"Good thing, because with all this snow, it's probably our only option unless you want to watch a movie."

Still comparing her adult life to her youth, Alicia admitted, "I can't remember the last time I played a board game."

Evelyn turned her attention to Alicia as she slid the pizza out of the oven and onto a hot pad. "Really? I play them at school with the kids sometimes."

"I should play more."

"Everyone should play more in my opinion." Evelyn handed her the pizza cutter and then topped off their wine glasses. "It's what's wrong with the world—all this work, work, work, and no play."

As they took their dinner back to the living room, Alicia considered Evelyn's comment. Alicia had laughed tonight, and she'd barely thought of her pain. Perhaps there was something to her friend's idea.

Chapter Nine

The next morning, the scent of butter and cinnamon woke Alicia from her slumber. She blinked a few times, noting her eyelids seemed to agree with the time. The change of location must have helped her to rest.

When she padded into the kitchen, she found a note from Evelyn saying she'd run out to get a few groceries and instructing her to enjoy the cinnamon rolls she'd baked for breakfast. Alicia lifted the towel covering the basket on the counter and the sugary aroma was heavenly. She pinched one, took it with her into the living room, and went over to the window.

She took a bite of the sticky confection and contemplated what a strange world this was. Every person's reality was completely different, yet they all existed together. While she'd been wallowing in misery back in Savannah, Evelyn had been inspiring students in this lovely little town, and Leo was getting his diner up and running. And while she and Evelyn were playing board games last night, Dean was... Where was he?

She zeroed in on the weekend crowds already filling the sidewalks and the stream of cars with out-of-state plates heading into town. Were all those people going to the bridge to change their lives? Like the world outside, the bridge was also unchanging. But people brought their hopes and dreams, their fears and worries. They called out for help or happiness or relief under that bridge. Could the miracles just be a shift in their thinking?

Alicia had experienced the shift firsthand, playing Scrabble with Evelyn. It was still her, but her thinking had changed. She'd slipped out of the grieving adult and into the playful girl she'd been. It wasn't a miracle, but her own doing.

"Miss me?" Evelyn asked, the door closing behind her after she walked in with a bag of groceries. She set it on the bar.

"I did, actually," Alicia said, turning around. "What are you doing for Christmas?"

Evelyn's brows rose. "I'm going to Mom and Dad's in the morning and then hanging out here. Why?"

"I scheduled my flight for next Friday, so I'm staying through the holiday. Want a housemate?" Alicia liked this part of herself she'd reconnected with, and she was happy to spend more time with her friend.

Evelyn clapped her hands together excitedly. "Absolutely! You can come with me to my parents' house if you want. They'd love to see you!"

After lunch, Evelyn and Alicia decided to drive down to Chapter and Verse, the local bookstore on Main Street, to look for a new read for the holiday.

"We should drive through the bridge today," Evelyn said as they got into her car.

"Why?"

"So I can make a request."

Alicia fastened her seat belt. "The bridge is probably a zoo on a Friday, and you know it has no power at all."

"I can't get Leo's dad out of my mind, and I want to do everything I can, even if that means asking for a miracle at the bridge."

"We don't need to waste our time with the old superstition of that bridge."

"Choose to believe the magic or not, but it doesn't hurt a thing to ask for Mr. Whitaker to be found safe. And maybe —just maybe—we'll be the next success story."

"All right," Alicia said, humoring her friend.

They drove through town and turned at the fork to head toward the bridge. As expected, they soon slowed due to the line of traffic clogging the route. Evelyn flicked on the radio to a station playing Christmas music, but for some reason the jovial tunes didn't fit with the atmosphere. All Alicia could think about was how each and every car held a need so great that the journey to the bridge was worth the drive. What turmoil lingered in each vehicle? Were people dealing with cancer diagnoses? Lost loved ones? Family problems? In a way, she didn't feel so isolated anymore, but at the same time, she realized the complexity of this life. No one had it easy. Not a single person.

When they'd finally reached the opening in the bridge, Alicia took in the greenery draped along the entrance, beckoning them inside with holiday cheer. Sure, it boasted its Christmas spirit, but how many hopes would never be realized?

Once they were under the shade of the bridge, Evelyn said, "Hey, Bridge. We're old friends, here. I've been visiting my whole life and I've got a big ask. Could you help us find

Dean Whitaker safe and sound? It might be the biggest gift you can give this season."

Alicia allowed her friend to send up her request, not believing it would help. But just before they drove out, with the gray winter light sliding across the dashboard, she offered up her own quick request: *I've already had one death to deal with. Please, don't give me two. I need a Christmas miracle for Dean.* They exited the bridge, and Alicia hung on to her appeal as they drove back to town.

At Chapter and Verse, the old oak floors creaked as the women entered, and the scents of ink and paper took Alicia back in time, clearing her mind of everything but the memories of this place during her childhood. The owner, Marty Simmons, raised his hand from behind the vintage counter and Alicia waved back. He didn't look the same as he had in his early thirties, but she could tell it was him by the point of his nose. He'd been the talk of the town gossips when he first bought the place at such a young age. People wondered if he'd come into some money or if he'd had bags of it stashed away his whole life. No one had ever answered that question for her definitively, and she'd forgotten all about him and the rumors until now.

"Oh! Let's play The Stacks," Alicia said to her friend.

Evelyn's face lit up. "I haven't played The Stacks with anyone since you left."

Alicia surveyed the few patrons in the shop and then eyed the tall bookshelves that stretched up to the original tin ceiling. "I'll take the front if you take the back."

"Okay," Evelyn said with a giggle. "But we don't have our notebooks."

"Just type it into your phone," Alicia directed.

She moved to the first alcove of books—the gently used section—and ran her finger along the spines of each of the novels, looking for a title she could use to build a sentence. The goal was to use three titles, all from books on the same shelf, to create a sentence before Evelyn could. The person without a sentence would buy the other's book that day.

Alicia tugged on a slightly battered copy of *The Bridges of Madison County* and pulled it out of the row just a bit so she could come back to it. Then she squinted at the books around it, none fitting her strategy. She'd never told Evelyn, but she always looked for titles that would give her two nouns and a verb. It worked every time.

At the end of the shelf, she tugged out *The Shack* from its spot, thinking "bridges" and "shack" might go together. Then she searched for a title with a verb on the same shelf. While looking, she formulated ideas for shacks and bridges to form her sentence. She pulled out her phone and quickly typed the two titles to make up for the time she spent searching for the third. There had to be a verb title on this shelf. If not, she'd have to abandon the two other books and move to another spot.

Then she found it. She pulled out *The Road Less Traveled* a tad and finished typing a sentence into her phone, the first thing that came to her: After enduring *The Bridges of Madison County*, she took *The Road Less Traveled* to *The Shack*.

"Done!" she called out, peeking around the shelf to the main aisle.

Marty jumped and then she caught the shift in his eyes as he seemed to remember their game.

"How do you find a sentence so quickly?" Evelyn asked, emerging from her aisle.

"I'll never give away my strategy." Alicia held out her phone so Evelyn could read. "They always just come to

100

me." Then she led Evelyn over to the bookshelf to show her the three books in question.

"Unbelievable."

Alicia laughed. "You don't actually have to buy my book, though."

"Oh, no. I have to. I lost The Stacks." She waved an arm around the shop. "Find a good one."

They spent the next hour perusing the shop. The large display window and the overstuffed chairs and sofas dotting Chapter and Verse made it a haven for booklovers. Alicia felt as if she'd come home after a long trip abroad, suddenly noticing all the little things that made her who she was. Every scuffed floorboard, the old oak shelves, the baldness of the wheels on the rolling ladder along one wall called to her as if their imperfections belonged with her somehow.

With a pile of books beside her, she snuggled into the Victorian-style antique sofa, the plum-colored velvet soft under her hands. She and Evelyn thumbed through their hopefuls, looking for that one book that would pull them in and not allow them to swim back out of it.

The shop hadn't changed much at all since the rainy days of her youth when she and Evelyn would drop their umbrellas at the door and rush to the teen section to spend their babysitting money. The shop seemed to cradle her as if to say, *"I'm here for you,"* and everything else faded away. Now she could fully remember why she'd rushed to the bridge that day so long ago and pleaded not to leave Noel, tears streaming down her teenage face.

"Are you going to be okay for a couple hours? I have to be at school early to get all the kids into costume," Evelyn said as they lumped their bags of books onto the chair in her apartment.

"Of course. I have tons to read."

"Want me to run back and pick you up?"

Alicia dug through her bag and pulled out a new mystery she'd bought. "That's silly. I can walk. It's not that far."

"You sure? It'll be getting dark by then."

"Well, maybe I can ask Leo. He could probably drive."

"Great idea. We'll invite him to dinner after."

With her mystery novel calling her, Alicia curled up on the sofa while Evelyn freshened up for the play. Before she knew it, her friend was on her way out again.

"See you tonight," she said before closing the door behind her.

Alicia waved and then finished the chapter she was reading. Then she texted Leo to ask if he could drive her to the play and to invite him to have dinner with her and Evelyn after. As she waited for his response, cocooned in the warmth of the little apartment, the Christmas tree sparkling in the corner, a wave of calm washed over her. She thought back to her condo in Savannah and understood why Bo had loved it more than she had. She enjoyed a more cozy, homey feel.

She decided to call her parents to check in and let them know her plans for the holiday.

"Helloooo," her mother answered.

"What are you up to?" Alicia asked.

"I'm covered in sand and nearly asleep in a beach chair. What are you doing?"

"Reading in Evelyn's apartment while she has play practice. We went to the bookstore earlier."

"Oh?"

"My flight was delayed due to the storm, so I'm going to spend Christmas with her."

"That sounds wonderful," her mother said through the static of wind blowing through the line. "How is Evelyn?"

"She's doing well. She's exactly the same," Alicia said, fondness for her friend making her smile. "She's got an apartment in the building they'd just started to renovate when we moved—right off of Main Street."

"Oh, yes. I remember. So what are you two going to do while you're there?"

"Tonight I'm going to watch a play at the middle school. She's the drama teacher."

"I can see that being a good fit for her," her mother said with a chuckle.

"Do you remember the old diner at the end of Main?"

"Yeah?"

"It's been completely redone. It's so nice. And the owner is going with me to the play. His name is Leo Whitaker. I met him my first night in Noel. He's new to town."

"That's wonderful." The hope in her mother's voice was thicker than maple syrup. "Let me know how it goes."

"I will."

"How about Christmas? Got any plans?"

"I think we're going to the Batons' for the day. Evelyn said they'd be happy to have me."

"I wish I could go with you. You know, your dad has had us hiking all over and he got us all tickets for zip-lining through the woods. He still thinks he's twenty-five. I told him he better not throw his back out."

Alicia laughed. "I've never known you—or him—to be the zip-lining type."

"I think it's a midlife crisis. It was either that or parasailing. Have you seen how high those things go?"

"Well, have fun."

She could almost feel the eye roll on the other end of the line.

"Call us later."

Alicia got off the phone, glad everything had worked out the way it had. She'd much rather spend time in Noel than zip-line across the humid Florida brush. She also noted that this was the first time since losing Bo that she actually had an opinion about what she'd *rather* do with her free time.

Her phone pinged with a text message from Leo. He said he could come get her and he'd love to go out to dinner after. A tiny spark lit inside her at spending the evening with him and her best friend.

Chapter Ten

Alicia climbed into Leo's purring vehicle, and they drove off to the middle-school play. The sun had dipped behind the mountains, leaving everything a pale blue outside.

"The snow hasn't gone anywhere," Leo said, maneuvering around a pile that hadn't been plowed enough to clear the lane. The weekend traffic had picked up on Main Street, and with the snow, the street was jammed.

"I know," she said as the cold slithered through her.

"I stopped by my house before coming to get you just to make sure Dad hadn't shown up." He steered around a turn, taking back roads to the school. "I wish it would warm up."

She understood now what people must have felt when she told them about her grief. She wanted to help Leo, to say something positive that would make the situation with his dad better, but there was nothing to say. They could spend all night looking for him and freezing, but if the search teams had had no luck, chances were they wouldn't either.

"Do you mind if we stop by my house again between the play and dinner? It probably won't amount to anything, but checking would give me some peace of mind."

"Of course."

Leo pulled into the almost full parking lot at the middle school. They got out and walked inside. As they made their way to the auditorium, Alicia felt as if she had stepped back in time. The old glazed-brick walls covered in artwork whisked her back to the years when she and Evelyn had skipped arm in arm down that hallway on their way to the bus after the school bell.

Alicia pointed to the junction between the gym and the cafeteria. "I used to wait for Evelyn on this corner after school."

Leo nodded, the brightness in his eyes letting her know that her nostalgia was catching.

"The teachers would call after us and tell us to slow down, but we'd go bounding to the bus most days, so happy to be together that we barely heard them."

They continued walking down the hallway, passing the trophy case full of the school's championship wins for cross-country, baseball, and lacrosse.

Alicia stopped at room 209 and peeked inside. "Oh, my goodness," she said, scanning the rows of desks and the board at the front of the room full of math problems. "This was my math class. I almost got a C one year because I was head over heels for Matthew Ramos and couldn't keep my mind on anything else."

Leo chuckled, pulling her attention to him. "What does Matthew Ramos do now?"

"I have no idea," she said with a laugh.

With every step they took, the memories flooded her and she gushed about it all to Leo.

"Over here is where I used to sit against the wall in the mornings, waiting for my friends. All the girls would collect in this spot and gossip before we went to class."

"What kinds of things did you gossip about?" Leo asked.

Alicia scanned her old memories, searching for an answer. "Oh! One time, we were certain that the English teacher Miss Johnson was dating our science teacher Mr. Callahan. Brittany Cash swore she saw them getting out of the same car in the parking lot one morning."

The corner of Leo's mouth turned upward in amusement. "Did you ever confirm it?"

She shook her head. "Not officially, but they arrived at the school picnic at the same exact time a week later, and we figured it had to be true."

They made it to the auditorium and went inside. About midway down the aisle, Leo gestured to two empty seats, and they sat down. The blue velvet curtain was still pulled shut on the stage with a single spotlight on the area where the two sides came together. The orchestra was setting up in rows of chairs near the stage, a couple of violins whining as their owners drew bows across the strings and eyed sheets of music in front of them. Evelyn paced across the stage and then disappeared behind the curtain.

"Was that your friend? She looked rushed."

"Yes. She's been here for two hours already. Hopefully everything is going okay."

Soon the lights dimmed and the chatting crowd quieted as the curtains whisked open to reveal a single child, dressed in black tails, a bow tie, and a top hat.

"Hello!" he greeted the crowd. "Tonight I bring you a chance to leave your holiday packages at the door and follow me into the past, present, and future."

Alicia settled into the story as the kids began entering

the stage, delivering their lines effortlessly. She caught sight of Evelyn standing in the corner at the edge of the curtain holding a clipboard and fluffing costumes before the kids walked on. They rolled the large wooden backgrounds in and out, and Evelyn had been right—they were very well painted.

The kids were fantastic, and before Alicia knew it, she'd fallen under the play's spell. For an hour and a half, she forgot where she was, immersed in the story. When the lights came on and the audience stood, cheering for the cast as they lined the stage, she and Leo followed suit. When everyone began to file out, they went into the hallway to wait for Evelyn.

The crowds dwindled, and her friend finally emerged. "What did you think?" she asked, beaming.

"It was adorable," Alicia replied. "What a wonderful performance from everyone. Wow."

"We only had one slight snafu when Kyle Bishop forgot his top hat. I had to run to the drama room and dig through the costume closet to find an alternative."

"No one was the wiser," Leo said.

"Thanks. But I'm afraid I need about forty-five minutes to finish up before dinner," Evelyn said.

"That's fine. Leo and I were going to run to his house really quickly. We can meet you."

"Shall we go to the diner for dinner?" Evelyn suggested. "I hear it has the best management in town." She winked at Leo.

He grinned. "Dinner's on me then. I'll text them to save us a table."

"All right. I'll meet you two there." Evelyn hurried off, stopping to say goodbye to one of the students and his family.

"Thank you for inviting me tonight," Leo said on their way to the car. "It was such a treat."

"You're welcome. It was good to have you here."

He sent a quick text, then they got into his SUV, and he pulled out of the parking lot. The old country lanes to Main Street were pitch-black. Alicia rubbed her cold hands together, glad she hadn't walked over. Leo switched on the radio, and Christmas carols filled the silence between them.

When the buzz of the play began to wear off, it occurred to her what their task was at this moment: they were on their way to check for Dean. And while she didn't want to be pessimistic, she was nearly certain they wouldn't find him safely inside. What would Christmas be like for Leo this year without his father? But, without Bo, she already knew. Her time in Noel had softened her grief, but she still wasn't sure what Christmas would bring.

They pulled onto Main Street and then headed out of town, taking the left-hand fork in the road.

"Oh, I used to live out this way," she said to make conversation.

"I bought a gorgeous piece of property about two miles down this road," Leo said.

"Wow, that will be *really* close to where I lived. What a coincidence."

As he continued driving, getting closer to her old home, she began to wonder. There weren't so many options out this way. When he turned into her old driveway, she laughed.

"You're not going to believe this," she said, "but this was my house."

Leo huffed his own laugh of disbelief as they got out. "Are you serious?"

"Yes. I grew up here." She pointed to the upstairs window. "That was my bedroom."

"Well, come on in. I'll show you around."

They walked up to the front door and he unlocked it, letting her inside. He reached around her and clicked on the lamp, and she took in the space, all her family's things replaced with his. It was as if she'd entered a new version of the gap, that gray space between now and never. Leather sofas sat where her parents' recliners had been, and the old TV on a cabinet filled with books had been swapped for a thin flat screen, mounted on the wall with a new fireplace underneath. A small Christmas tree stood next to the window. The echoes of her life here lingered in her subconscious, but the reality had changed.

"I've been too busy to decorate much for the holiday," Leo said.

She waved toward the tree. "It's nice."

"I didn't even put up stockings or wrap the Christmas presents," he said with a remorseful shake of his head. "I should have. For Dad."

"Don't beat yourself up."

He shrugged.

She followed him down the dark hallway and he flipped on the light in the kitchen. The cabinets had been upgraded, and the sleek iron lighting was more masculine than Mama's had been. Leo walked over to the kitchen window and peered out into the darkness.

"My dad liked this house because of the view," he said. "That's why we bought it. But now I fear it might have swallowed him." He turned on the light outside, illuminating the backyard.

It was hard to imagine the woods she'd loved causing harm to someone. When she was growing up, the canopy of trees, the small streams meandering through the valleys, the way the summer sun filtered through the branches—it had all felt like her personal playground, as if it protected her from the world. Her memory of this wide expanse of woods seemed so big and almighty that it made whatever powers people thought the bridge had seem silly.

Leo opened the back door, letting in a rush of cold air. The barren tree line seemed to be expressing its sadness for the situation, the spindling limbs reaching out as if asking for a hug. *Where is Dean?* That question had rolled around in her subconscious since she'd heard he'd gone missing. It was the first thing in her mind each morning and the last thing before she fell asleep. She tried to force herself to hold on to hope the way Leo was, but life just didn't seem that kind in her experience.

"He really likes watching the birds in that birdhouse out there." Leo directed her attention to the cedar box nailed to the oak tree out back.

"I made that birdhouse," she said, delighted it was still there. "My dad helped me nail it to the tree, and we kept it filled with birdseed to attract the birds."

"They still show up. I should get some birdseed. That's a great idea."

"I used to watch them from the kitchen window in the mornings."

He shut the door. "Want to see the rest of the house?"

"Yes," she replied. Although the home was so different now that the four walls containing her room didn't seem to matter so much anymore.

Leo led her around, showing her the dining area first.

"We used to have big Thanksgiving dinners here," she said, stepping into the room. "Instead of a round table like you have, we had a huge rectangular table. We'd bring in all the chairs from the kitchen, and my aunts and uncles gathered around with us. We ate and Mama and my aunts cleared until dessert was done, and then we'd get out a deck of cards and play until the football games came on."

Leo smiled. "Where do you all have Thanksgiving now?"

"We haven't really gotten together with everyone much since we moved from Noel. My family is all spread out now."

"It seems like a shame not to get together. I've always wanted a big family, but it's just me and my dad for now."

She swallowed. She was wasting precious time by not seeing her family more. She decided she'd make a point to see them after she got home. Maybe after they all came home from Florida they'd like to get together again when she could join them.

Leo took her around the rest of the house and then upstairs to her room, which was now half a study and half a guest room. "I haven't done much with this one."

She walked over to the closet door and ran her fingers over the holes in the grain. "I used to have a full-length mirror right here. I'd put on music and dance in front of it."

"Did it help?"

She looked at him. "Help?"

"Did practicing in front of the mirror help you dance better? I've heard that it does."

"I'm not sure," she said with a laugh. "But I'd use the end of my jump rope as a microphone." The memories flowed through her easily tonight. And the more she immersed herself in her old life, the more authentic that part of her felt.

Leo laughed. "Well, I guess we should head on to dinner," he said.

"Yeah, we probably should."

They went downstairs and Leo made sure the back door was unlocked before they left. "Just in case," he said, leaving the light on out back.

Then they got back into his SUV and drove toward town.

Chapter Eleven

When Alicia and Leo met Evelyn at the diner, every table was bustling with families, groups of people immersed in jovial conversation, and waitstaff rushing to the kitchen and back.

"Busy night," Evelyn said, ducking under Leo's arm as he held the door open for them.

"The bridge visitors start trickling in on Thursday evening, and by Friday night, it's standing room only at the old counter-turned-bar, with every table occupied." He nodded to the frazzled hostess who offered him an exhausted smile. "Not to worry, they saved us a table in the back."

The hostess gathered three menus and took them to the corner of the dining area, where sat what looked to be the last empty booth, and they slid onto the benches, the women on one side with Leo on the other.

"Hanging in there, Tiff?" Leo asked the hostess.

"Yes, sir. Katelyn's got this table tonight, so she'll be over in a second."

After she left, Leo leaned in toward Alicia and Evelyn.

"It's not much of an incentive, but I let the staff take home a dish of their choice after we close on Fridays. The crowds are running them ragged, and I need to hire more servers, but I've been spending all my free time looking for my dad."

"No news when you got home?" Evelyn asked.

Leo shook his head.

"You'll never believe where he and his father live," Alicia said.

Evelyn offered a questioning frown.

"My old house—316 Radnor Lane."

"Leo owns your house?" Evelyn asked with a gasp.

Alicia nodded. "And he said his dad likes the birdhouse I made out back."

"Oh, gosh, I'd forgotten about that. We used to add birdseed to it after school."

The waitress arrived and took their drink orders. She asked if they were ready to put in their dinner choices, but Leo asked for a few more minutes.

"Evelyn and I spent every day after school in the woods behind my house," Alicia said once the waitress had gone. "My parents were worried we'd get lost."

"Rightfully so," Leo said.

Alicia nodded solemnly. "Yeah, we know now. But as kids, we had no idea what could happen to us. When I was in the woods, I felt free."

"Me too," Evelyn said. "Remember how we followed the brook that ran through the valley? It opened up into a wider stream, and we'd take off our shoes so we could walk on the mossy rocks. We pretended it was carpet."

"Oh, yeah, that's right."

"It sounds like you two had fun out there."

"We did," Evelyn said with a nostalgic look in her eye.

"It's such a vast forest. You never got lost?" Leo asked.

115

Alicia shook her head, but Evelyn held up a finger.

"No, once we got lost. Remember?" Evelyn put her elbows on the table and her brows pulled together as if she was trying to retrieve the memory. "That one time when we were out after dark... We walked along the stream for hours that day, winding through the mountains. Oh, and we discovered that old shack! We got so excited we didn't start back home until sundown."

The memory slowly materialized for Alicia. "Ooh, yeah. I had completely forgotten we found that. It had dirty old pots and pans and things, right? We stayed all day and pretended it was our house."

Evelyn's smile widened. "Yes! We made brooms from sticks and evergreens and swept the floors. We tried to clean the pots and utensils in the water outside, and we even tried to make a fire in the old stone fireplace. Thank God we didn't actually make one or we might have burned down the entire mountain."

"There was a fireplace?" Leo asked.

"Yes," Evelyn replied. "And a basin for washing. It was next to a spot where the brook widened into a rushing current. It was so pretty."

"Wait," Alicia said, stopping them both. "It was behind my old house—your house. And an outdoorsman would know how to build a fire to keep warm." She peered into Leo's wide eyes, that tiny spark of hope flickering.

"How far is it?" he asked.

"It's hard to remember... so much time has passed, and we were kids taking our time... What do you think, Evelyn? Maybe a little over an hour's walk if we hurried?"

"Maybe," Evelyn replied.

Leo's shoulders rose. "Do you think you'd remember how to get there?"

Alicia folded her arms on the table and scanned her memory, trying to recall the exact path. "I'm not sure... We followed the brook. It was some time ago, but as long as the water hasn't dried up or gotten covered in snow, we could probably find it again."

"I'll go tonight," he said, moving to stand up.

But Alicia caught his arm. "Leo, you can't go in the dark." She shook her head. "It would be dangerous, and the temperatures are too low."

"I can manage."

Alicia pulled on his arm to get him to sit and he complied. "The mountain terrain is so unsteady, and with nothing more than a flashlight to guide you, you'd get lost yourself and freeze to death. I'll go with you first thing in the morning."

"I'll come too, if you want," Evelyn said. "Between the two of us, we could probably find it."

For the rest of the dinner, they made plans for the hiking trip the next morning.

"I'll let the staff know I won't be in tomorrow. We could start at six," Leo said. "That would get us out there around sunrise."

"We'll need to dress warm," Alicia worried aloud. "I'm not sure I have what I'll need."

"Don't worry about that," Evelyn cut in. "I go skiing every year. We're about the same size, and I have a couple pairs of ski pants."

"That's wonderful," Alicia said with relief. "How about you, Leo?"

"I'm from Chicago—very cold winters. I've got what I need. I also have warmers we can put in our gloves and socks. They last about ten hours."

Alicia was hopeful and reached out to Bo. She hadn't

done that since she'd left Savannah, but she sent up a silent prayer.

Bo, if you have any pull with the big guy upstairs—I don't even know if you can hear me—but I'm gonna need the biggest miracle you can manage. Please help us find Dean.

Bo would certainly be better help than that old bridge.

Suddenly, she gasped when a thought popped into her mind.

"What is it?" Evelyn asked.

Leo looked on.

A cold wave slithered through Alicia's body. She shook her head, not wanting to believe what was going through her mind. "Nothing." She grabbed the salt. "I almost knocked this over with my elbow."

What she didn't want to mention was that they'd asked to find Dean at the bridge today. And in the bookstore she'd created the sentence: After enduring *The Bridges of Madison County*, she took *The Road Less Traveled* to *The Shack*. Could her sentence actually mean something? There was only one way to find out.

Alicia thought about the message the whole way back to Evelyn's apartment. And when they got home after dinner, Evelyn was still abuzz from their dinner planning. Her friend grabbed the plate of cookies they'd made and they sat down on the sofa together.

"I have to tell you something that occurred to me," Alicia finally said. "I didn't want to get Leo's hopes up, but it's been on my mind since dinner."

Evelyn offered her a cookie. "What?"

As she took one of the sweet confections, the tingle of optimism swelled. "Remember our sentences when we played The Stacks in the bookshop?"

"Yeah." Evelyn broke a piece of cookie and popped it into her mouth.

"I linked the wish at the bridge to the sentence I'd made." She repeated it and Evelyn threw her hand over her mouth, eyes wide.

"What if the bridge's magic actually works?" Evelyn asked.

"It doesn't work until we find Dean."

The old man had gone too many days without food, and she wasn't sure how he'd be equipped to camp for so long. He'd only left to go on a walk, as far as they were aware. Her enthusiasm gave way to the dread of the disappointment they'd all have if they didn't recover Leo's father. And they still had to *find* the shack. It had been years. Would they remember how to get there? And if they did manage to locate it, was the structure even still standing?

Their conversation dwindled as they sank into their thoughts. Soon Alicia went to bed, her sentence from the bookstore dancing in her mind.

Chapter Twelve

Dressed in borrowed ski pants the next morning, Alicia lifted a large backpack onto her back. She and Evelyn had stuffed it full of supplies—a blanket, two thermoses of water, a few snacks, and a first aid kit. As the women left Evelyn's apartment and drove to Leo's, a quiet hum of anticipation filled the air.

They pulled up to Alicia's childhood home and got out of the car. Their breaths puffed in front of them, the frigid wind burning Alicia's cheeks. They both seemed to notice the difficult conditions. It would be a very cold hour-plus trek through the wilderness.

"I've got everything packed." Leo's voice pulled Alicia's attention to the door. He was wearing a ski mask with the hood of his thick coat secured tightly below his chin. "Anyone need to use the restroom before we get going?"

"I'm good," Alicia said, walking up to meet him.

Evelyn shook her head. "I'm fine too."

"Okay, come on inside and let's put warmers in our boots and gloves."

With quick, efficient movements, they began working

the small warming pouches into their boots. Evelyn looked around at the décor, but didn't say anything. They were there for a mission.

As they trudged through the thick snow, Alicia locked eyes with Leo. While the rest of his face was hidden by the ski mask, she deciphered the purpose and determination in his gaze and understood completely. They plodded toward the forest, and she was glad to be there for him, to be doing something to help, no matter what happened.

She and Leo seemed to have a connection, a dynamic she'd never experienced with anyone else. Neither overshadowed the other, and they complemented each other in a way she and Bo hadn't. There was a natural balance to their conversation, and she respected how he'd changed his whole life for his dad. She understood putting others before herself—she did that every day with her work as a nurse. Walking beside him felt right. Even though she didn't know what they might face today, she was ready as long as she was by his side.

The only sounds around them were their breaths and the crunch of their boots in the icy snow. A few miles down the road, people were window-shopping, buying gingerbread lattes, and enjoying the holiday season in town. Cars were most likely lined up to drive through the bridge, and then the families would settle in the area's cafés and restaurants while Christmas music played.

Out there in the woods, the holiday was the furthest thing from her mind. This was a rescue mission, one possibly final chance to find Leo's dad. Whatever they found—or didn't—would impact Christmas for all three of them forever, Alicia was certain.

She pushed away the worry. She couldn't focus on that.

They reached the tree line and wound down the hillside toward the brook. The terrain grew steeper, with the snow hiding potential stumbling blocks. Her center of gravity seemed off compared to the feeling she had when running through the area as a child. She tripped and Leo grabbed her arm, his boots sliding on the loose rock.

"You okay?" he asked.

"Yeah."

Evelyn stayed nearer to Alicia, as if they'd be safer in closer proximity. "I don't remember the woods being this difficult to hike when we were kids. How would an old man walk this?" she asked.

"It's usually flatter, but the snow is drifting," Alicia replied. "Dean would've walked the trail with no problem if the snow hadn't fallen yet."

Leo, still silent, plodded ahead of them, creating a wider trail by moving fallen limbs to the side and breaking off any of the twigs that jutted out in their pathway. They continued until the forest floor evened out, the gap between the trees on either side of the path becoming more visible. As they crunched through the snow, Alicia pulled her scarf over her nose and mouth to protect her face from the freezing wind.

Soon a gurgle drew them to a small clearing. Alicia's pulse quickened.

"The brook," she said, pointing to the snaking stream of water and ice that trailed west through the forest.

The three hikers moved toward the water in unison. Alicia was already cold, and they probably had more than an hour to go. With every step, she worried what they might discover when they got to the shack. *If* they found it.

The area was still vaguely familiar, even buried in snow. This had been the playground of Alicia's childhood.

Despite the cold, the protective feeling that the woods had given her back then enveloped her today.

"I remember now," Evelyn said, breaking the silence. "We went up that hill and through the valley where the stream splits."

"Yes, you're right," Alicia said.

She struggled to get through another drift, her boots no match for the thick snow. Leo came up behind her and lifted her over the bank, then he helped Evelyn. Alicia didn't have long to think about his touch before she faced the fork in the stream.

Evelyn pointed up the hill. "This way."

They kept going for what felt like hours, but ended up being only about fifty minutes when she checked her watch. She remembered the sense of a loss of time from when she was a kid. Out there, the minutes stood still, and the world faded away. It was just her and the trees—no rules, no schedules.

Alicia could barely feel her nose, and her hands and feet were cold despite the warmers. It would be tough to make the walk back, but if they found Dean, it would be worth it. Although, how would they get him back to the house in all this snow if, by some miracle, he was there? Worst case, someone could stay with him until they could alert an emergency crew to the location.

Leo's breath billowed in front of him. Snow had started falling again. He hadn't said much during the journey. He was likely teetering between that last shred of faith that they'd find Dean alive and, well, the absolute panic that they wouldn't. Or something even worse... They didn't know what they were walking into. This was his family, the man who'd raised him. The man he'd changed his entire life for.

After another twenty or so minutes—she'd lost track—
an old shack came into view. Her heart pounded. The small
stone chimney had no smoke rising from it, which meant no
fire was burning inside. That wasn't a good sign, but maybe
her mind was playing tricks on her. She kept coming up
with plausible scenarios. Perhaps the fire had been going
and warmed the room and Dean let it die down. Or maybe
in the whiteness of all the snow, they just couldn't see the
smoke. She tried not to think about how all the wood was
wet from the storm and wouldn't burn even if Dean was
there and could start the fire.

Leo bounded up to the door and grabbed the handle,
wrenching the door open. "Dad?"

When Alicia and Evelyn reached the shack, a gray light
filtered through the tree branches, settling on the wooden
floor of the structure's porch. Alicia peeked her head inside
the doorway and winced at the pungent smell. Once it was
clear that no one was there, Leo walked into the one-room
shack and the women followed. He dug around in his bag
and pulled out a small lantern and a matchbook, then lit the
lantern and set it on the small table. The wood in the fireplace had all burned down to ash. Luckily, a small pile of
dry wood was stacked to the side of the fireplace. Leo
grabbed a handful and arranged it in the hearth before
working to light it. No one said a word as he used match
after match, trying to set fire to the kindling. Disappointment hung in the air like a heavy fog.

When the fire finally got going, the three of them,
exhausted from the hike, stood close to it and warmed their
frozen limbs while the snow continued falling outside.
Alicia took her gloves off and tossed them on the table. She
held her pink fingers out toward the flame to warm them.
The heat spread through her, burning her icy skin.

Once she'd warmed up, she allowed herself to observe the space. It seemed as though lots of people had stopped to rest in the shelter. A forgotten sweatshirt lay in a lump in one corner, covered by leaves that must have blown in when the door had been left open. A few old pans looked as if they'd recently been used to cook fish, which was most certainly the source of the smell. Litter was strewn about as well—discarded food wrappers, old cigarette butts, and bits of fishing line.

"Looks like another dead end," Leo finally said, frustration clear in his solemn expression.

Evelyn leaned against the wall and tipped her head back.

Apparently the sentence Alicia had made playing The Stacks had meant nothing after all. She should have figured.

"I say we stay as long as we can stomach the smell so we're good and warm, then we'll make our way back," said Leo. "I can try to scrape the trout out of the pan and rinse it off in the stream. The water's not entirely frozen in this spot."

"I can manage the smell," Alicia said, not wanting to put him through the trouble of freezing just to wash out a cast-iron pan. "The sulfur from the matches helped."

"I'm fine too," Evelyn said.

"Well, you two can be heroes if you want to, but I'm about to be sick from the stench." He took the pan and slipped out the door, taking most of the smell with him.

"I can't believe Mr. Whitaker isn't here," Evelyn said after Leo had gone. "I would've bet money that he'd be here. I felt it in my bones."

"It's so discouraging. He could have stayed warm here."

Evelyn took off her gloves as well and warmed her

hands next to Alicia. "I feel terrible for Leo. It must be so upsetting."

"I can't imagine." At least Alicia had answers about Bo. Would Leo ever definitively know what happened to his dad?

Leo soon came back inside, covered in newly fallen snow, and put the rinsed pan on the table. He pulled his ski mask down under his chin. "Are you two thawing out?"

"Nearly," Alicia said as she stepped aside and motioned for Leo to come closer to the fire. He'd yet to stay still and get warm.

Feeling better, she moved over to the table to allow him more space, but she stumbled on a warped floorboard. She put her hand on the table to catch herself.

"Ow!" she yelled when something sharp poked her finger. Bright red blood bubbled on her skin.

"What happened?" Evelyn said, turning around.

"I tripped." She pointed to the floorboard. "When I caught myself, a nail must have jabbed me."

"Have you had a tetanus shot recently?" Leo asked.

"Yeah. For work." Alicia was already digging through her backpack with one hand.

"That's good," Evelyn said, helping her. She pulled out the first aid kit and got a cleaning wipe, a bandage, and some ointment. "Here, hold out your finger."

Alicia complied and Evelyn got her finger cleaned and bandaged.

"Be careful," Alicia warned as she looked around for the nail that had stabbed her. She brushed a few leaves aside when something silver caught her eye. "Oh," she said, plucking it up. "It was a fishing lure. I should've guessed, given the trout that was left behind." She held it out to Leo. "Need an extra?"

He only half looked, his mind clearly elsewhere, but then he spun back and snatched it from her hand. He sucked in a deep breath and then blew hot air onto the lure and wiped it on his shirt. His eyes became glassy and his chest heaved with short breaths. He turned it around and showed them the inscription: a large W with an R and a D on either side.

"Richard Dean Whitaker," he said. "I got him this specialty lure for his birthday about four years ago."

Evelyn gasped.

"He's been here," Alicia whispered.

In one stride, Leo had crossed the small space and flung open the door. "Dad!" he called out into the woods, marching through the snow coming down so fast it caused a whiteout around them.

"Dad!" He rushed down to the stream. "Dad!"

Alicia pulled her gloves back on and ran outside with him. Evelyn followed. Alicia tried to listen, but nothing surfaced except for the sound of the moving water.

"How long do you think that fish had been here?" she asked Leo.

"I don't know. Dad!" he called again.

"I'm guessing a couple days," Evelyn said. "But, by the smell, it could have been longer."

Leo continued to yell for his father, so Alicia started calling for him as well. But it had likely been long enough since he'd caught the fish that if Dean had been able to keep going, he wasn't anywhere near them. Still, she continued calling for Leo's sake.

"Dean? Mr. Whitaker? Are you here?"

"He's not here, but he was," Leo said, hope glistening in his eyes.

"The snow is really coming down," Evelyn said. "We

should probably head back soon. It's already tough to know how long to follow the stream to get back. Everything's starting to look the same."

Leo put his hands over his eyes to shield them and looked in every direction. "I don't want to leave if he's been here."

"We'll go straight to the sheriff's department and show them what we discovered," Alicia suggested. "Now they have a search area, and they can fan out with more equipment and manpower." She took his arm. "We should definitely head back."

"All right." Leo grabbed a handful of snow, went inside the shack, and threw it on the fire to smother it.

They began the hike back to his house, each quiet for different reasons. The buzz of excitement bounced around between them, the sound of their steps drowned out by the howl of the wind. Alicia barely felt the cold anymore. All she could think about was how her sentence from The Stacks might have saved Leo's dad.

Chapter Thirteen

By the time they made it back to Leo's house, the snow was coming down too hard to drive, so Leo called the sheriff's office. While he was on the phone in the kitchen explaining what they'd found, Alicia and Evelyn stripped off their outerwear. Thank goodness Alicia's jeans under her ski pants were dry.

"What are the odds that he lives in *your* house?" Evelyn whispered.

"I know. It's such a coincidence." Alicia wrapped herself in one of the blankets Leo had left on the couch for her and Evelyn, and dropped to the floor close to the fire.

Evelyn sat down next to her. "I don't think there are any coincidences in life."

"What? There are plenty."

Evelyn shook her head. "I think they all mean something. That's why the bridge is so famous. People can see the messages in the coincidences."

Alicia laughed, charmed by her friend's optimism. "What makes you think every serendipitous instance has meaning?"

"If Leo didn't live here, we wouldn't have known where to look for his dad. We wouldn't have gotten evidence that the search parties hadn't even unearthed. Don't you think that was meant to be?"

"I think it was lucky," Alicia said, although she had to admit that a lot of people certainly had experienced things they couldn't explain in relation to the bridge. Had one of their requests had something to do with this latest development?

She sifted through all the things that had happened since she'd arrived in Noel. Her yearning to hear Bo, and then Leo saying the one thing her fiancé would've said. Bo's voice came back to her once more. *"I knew this would happen."* It gave her a shiver. Then she'd been in the hospital with her old friend at the same time the sheriff was there looking for Dean, and Tabitha could explain what had happened. And now she sat in her childhood home, one step closer to finding the older man. Had it all been some sort of miraculous response to their prayers at the bridge? A part of her wanted to believe it.

"They said the conditions aren't safe to send people out searching today," Leo said as he walked into the room, "but they're going to start calling all the homes on that side of the valley. It's a different county that we haven't checked yet. Maybe someone's seen him."

"I hope so," Alicia said, still trying to get rid of the chill.

"Maybe he got a ride somewhere," Evelyn said. "Is there anywhere you can think of that he'd want to go?"

They'd moved from the floor to the couch and were both wrapped up like burritos on each end.

Leo shook his head and rubbed the dark stubble on his chin. "I've tried. For the life of me, I can't think of anywhere he wanted to go. The diner was his dream and he wanted to be there all the time. He'd have shown up if he could."

"I want to believe he's somewhere safe," Evelyn said. "I feel it in my gut."

"We can hope." Leo picked up the lure from the table and peered at it, then set it back down. "Well, we're not getting out again to look for him any time soon, and I'm afraid you're both stuck here. Might as well make yourselves at home." He grabbed the remote and turned on the TV, then handed it to Alicia. "I can make us all a cup of coffee, if you'd like. Or some soup. Anyone hungry?"

"Yes, thank you," Evelyn said with a grateful nod.

Alicia passed the remote to Evelyn and then adjusted her blanket so she could stand. "I'll help you."

They went into the kitchen, and Leo filled the coffee pot with water.

"Okay, making coffee in my old house... This is kind of fun." She pointed to the cabinet. "Mugs still in here?"

He smiled despite the day's tension. "Yep."

She opened it and pulled out three, then lined them up on the counter. "I suppose it's a good cabinet for mugs, since it's above the plug for the coffee maker." She pointed to the drawer by the sink. "Silverware?"

His brows pulled together. "Are we really that predictable as a species that we can't even choose our own silverware drawer?"

"We're not predictable. We're resourceful," Alicia said. "The silverware drawer is the closest drawer to the dishwasher, and we all know how annoying it would be to carry all that clean cutlery across the kitchen when we unload it."

The corner of his mouth arched up. "I can't say I was thinking about that when I unpacked. But from my old habits working in kitchens, I do suppose I chose that drawer because it was the widest for my kitchen knives. I don't like them piled on top of one another."

"So subconsciously you were more aware than you thought you were."

Alicia was unused to being the positive one, at least lately, thinking they all had some underlying force driving them. Before this trip, she'd been convinced that everything happened at face value. But was there a bigger picture in the making? Being here in this town, with these people, had done something for her that she couldn't put her finger on.

Leo loaded the coffee maker and hit start. Alicia tightened the blanket around her shoulders. The kitchen had always been drafty.

"Are you warm enough?" Leo asked.

"I'll be fine."

The snow continued falling out the window. She hadn't seen anything like this storm when she'd lived there. It seemed never-ending.

A cardinal flew into her line of sight and landed on a nearby branch.

"Look," she whispered to Leo as she pointed to the bird. "Isn't it beautiful?"

Leo set a container of creamer on the counter and joined her, leaning forward to peer out the window. "When I was a little boy, my mother used to tell me that our loved ones who'd passed on would visit us on the wings of a cardinal."

"Oh," she said, looking out at the bird. Could the story be true? Perhaps the cardinal was Leo's mother. She certainly hoped it wasn't Dean. Or maybe it was Bo. Could he be watching over her?

The coffee maker beeped just after the bird flew off, breaking the spell. She snapped herself back to reality.

Leo pulled out a wooden tray from under a lower cabinet, filled it with three bowls, and heated up a couple of cans of soup while Alicia went into the living room to ask Evelyn what she wanted in her coffee. When she got back, Leo was on the phone, pacing the kitchen.

"When?" he asked.

Alicia began to pour the coffee, her hands moving slower than usual as she attempted to figure out why the caller had Leo's face so concerned.

"Is there anything we can do today?" His gaze fell upon Alicia, but he didn't seem to register her presence, his thoughts entirely on the call.

She added cream to the coffees and stirred.

"All right. Call me any time if you find out more." Leo ended the call, leaned against the counter, and exhaled loudly.

Evelyn was now standing in the doorway. "Is everything okay?"

Leo turned his focus to Alicia and his lips parted as if the words were stuck in his throat. Then his astonished look began to lift. "Somebody across the valley thinks they saw Dad yesterday."

Alicia gasped and Evelyn rushed in.

"How do they know it was him?" Alicia asked.

"A farmer was out plowing snow and saw an older man cut through a field at the edge of his property and head into the trees. He was wearing the coat and boots that match Dad's description, and he was carrying fishing gear and a blanket."

"That's incredible," Alicia said.

"The farmer tried to find him, but couldn't." Leo erupted with a loud *whoop* and pumped his fist in the air, then slammed it onto the counter loudly and broke into a wild laugh. "Ha-ha! I can't believe it! He made it through!"

Evelyn let out an excited squeal.

A new feeling ran through Alicia's veins. She wasn't sure how to describe it. Ever since Bo died, nothing had seemed right in her world. She wasn't sure she'd believed Dean could be alive because to her mind, the world wasn't kind enough for that. But now there was evidence he might have made it through the storm, and while he wasn't safe by any means, something was helping him. She thought back to the cardinal she'd seen. It had come just before this news. Before this week, she never would have believed that a random bird sighting would have a thing to do with her reality, but now she wasn't so sure. Had her life begun to change as a result of her visiting the bridge in Noel? Or was she just falling for the myth like everyone else?

"Do you think he's still finding shelter in the shack?" Evelyn asked.

"They're trying to see if they can send an officer out on a snowmobile. Getting equipment for all this snow has been tough. They aren't prepared for it. I told them I wanted to go back out and wait for Dad at the shack, but they advised me to stay here in case he returns to the house. The sheriff said it's too dangerous to go back into the woods without proper precautions."

Alicia sent up a silent prayer. *If all of this is real, we need the snow to stop so we can get to Dean. Bo, if you're up there, please put in a good word for us.*

For the rest of the day, Leo, Alicia, and Evelyn operated under a buzz of excitement. The TV was on and the fire blazed as they spent the afternoon chatting. Their conversation moved from topic to topic, yet Alicia was sure they were all silently wondering where Dean was at that moment. As they talked, a strange sort of calm settled in the air, despite the fact that Dean was yet to be located. They were all just so relieved he'd made it through the worst of the storm.

While the sun set, Alicia prayed they'd find him before the plunging temperatures returned. The fact that he'd made it this far gave her faith that he could manage until he was brought home.

"You said your dad's favorite time of year is Christmas," Alicia said after a few minutes of quiet, a new sense of faith coming over her. Their luck so far had given her hope that if any holiday could be a great one, it would be this Christmas. "What if he comes home as a Christmas miracle?"

"I'd thank God every day for the rest of my life," Leo said.

Evelyn scooted to the edge of the sofa. "Christmas is about believing, right?"

Leo nodded.

"What if we *believe*? What if we prepare for his arrival as if we *know* he's coming? What if we push away all doubts from our minds?"

"It can't hurt," Alicia agreed. "Get those stockings you wanted to put up, Leo. Let's wrap the presents and finish decorating. What's the worst that could happen if we do— you have a festive, cozy house? Best-case scenario, the Christmas cheer will be waiting for Dean when he shows up."

"You've got a point," Leo said. "He'd be overjoyed by a gesture like that. And I've said I'll do anything to bring him home. I even wished inside a bridge. What could a few stockings hurt?"

Alicia smiled. "Exactly."

"We need to get in the mood." Evelyn clapped her hands excitedly. "Let's put on some Christmas music. And we should bake cookies! It's not Christmas without cookies."

Leo went over to the radio and tuned it to a holiday station. "Evelyn, do you mind rooting through the pantry to see if I have what we need to make cookies? I'm not sure if I have everything... I know I have flour, sugar, and butter."

"You were an executive chef, and you aren't sure if you have basic ingredients for cookies?" Alicia teased him.

"What can I say? I don't bring my work home." A mixture of amusement and fondness sparkled in his eyes.

Alicia laughed.

"Not to worry—I'm on it!" Evelyn hopped up from the sofa and ran into the kitchen.

"I'll get the rest of the Christmas decorations. Alicia, want to help me?" Leo asked.

"Of course."

"Grab your coat. It's cold in the attic."

She put on her coat and followed him up the flight of stairs. Leo flipped on the light when they entered the attic. The cold air gave her a chill and she sent up another prayer for Dean.

"I can't imagine how your dad is staying warm in this storm with only a coat and blanket."

"When we got there, it looked like the fire had been lit," Leo said. "And someone cooked that fish. Knowing him, I'll bet he had matches in his fishing gear. He probably has a first aid kit and snacks too. He was always prepared."

Alicia smiled.

Leo sat on the top step of the attic and dug through one of the boxes. "When I was a kid, he used to take me fishing for the day, but his fishing trips weren't like most."

Alicia sat next to him.

"He filled the back of his truck with supplies. When we found the perfect spot—out of the way and in the shade—he put up this big tent he had, and then snapped open a folding table where he sat three boxes: one was his fishing box, the other two were snacks."

"That sounds like fun," Alicia said, forgetting about the cold.

"He and I would scavenge the woods for big rocks so we could make a circle for a fire pit. Then we'd cook hot dogs, s'mores, whatever he brought."

Leo's gaze fell on the wall of the attic, but it was clear by the glisten in his eyes that he was lost in thought. "For my sixth birthday, he took me fishing, and in the back of his truck was a massive tire. He sat me down on the edge of the river bank, in one of his foldable camping chairs, and gave me a baited fishing pole and a soda. Then he spent the next hour hanging a tire swing from a nearby oak tree. Once it was up, the two of us took turns swinging over the river and dropping into the ice-cold water. If I close my eyes, I can still remember the sound of his laugh right before the splash."

"What a sweet story," Alicia said. "Thank you for telling me."

"I haven't thought about his younger days in ages. I don't know what made me think of that particular moment." He twisted toward her. "Maybe it was you being here. I'm so glad you came to the diner the other night."

Her heart pattered. Leo reminded her that she was still

alive. She didn't feel left behind when she was with him. "I'm glad too."

"I've been working so hard on getting the diner up and running that I hadn't gotten to know anyone, so when Dad went missing, I felt alone. Until you showed up."

"I understand," she said. "I felt the same way."

"Where did you say you're from?" he asked.

"Georgia."

"When do you fly back?"

"Friday." Sitting in the cold attic with Leo, she didn't want to be anywhere else. Going back to her empty condo and the shell of the life she'd been building with Bo seemed unimaginable.

Leo didn't say anything else, both of them seemingly lost in their own thoughts.

What should I do? A gust of wind blew through the vent at the roofline, making Alicia shiver. She put her hands in the pockets of her coat, and her fingers brushed a folded piece of paper in one of them. She took it out and opened it.

"What's that?" Leo asked.

"It's the volunteer form from the hospital. The front desk clerk asked me to sign up when I stopped by. She didn't know I was leaving." She peered down at the form, the blank lines calling to her. "I wonder if they need any help with all the snow."

"We can dig out the car tomorrow, and if we can get on the road, I could take you over. You've still got a week. They might appreciate an extra set of hands if nurses are having trouble getting there in the snow."

"I'd love that." She folded the paper and put it back in her pocket. "Thank you."

"I'd be happy to."

They locked eyes.

"Well, let's get you down before you freeze." Leo hoisted a box in his arms. "Ready?"

She nodded.

When they got downstairs, Alicia took off her coat and went into the kitchen. Evelyn had her hands in a large bowl. "We didn't have chocolates for chocolate chip cookies, but I found butter, sugar, eggs, vanilla, flour, and baking soda." She flashed a wide smile. "That will make a basic sugar cookie."

Leo came in and leaned around Alicia's shoulder. "Wow. I actually had what you needed. That's a Christmas miracle in itself."

"You don't, by chance, have any cookie cutters, do you?" Evelyn asked.

Leo laughed. "A house with two bachelors? Definitely not."

"That's perfectly fine. I can shape them without one."

"You're incredible," Alicia said, giving her friend a squeeze.

Evelyn wrinkled her nose playfully. "Thank you." She pulled her doughy hands from the bowl. "How's the decorating?"

"We're just about to start," Leo said as he opened the fridge. He pulled out a bottle of white wine. "My staff got me this for Christmas and I've been wondering when I would ever drink it. I think tonight is a good night. What do you two think?"

"That sounds wonderful," Alicia said.

"Yes, I'd love some," Evelyn chimed in while she washed batter off her hands at the sink.

Leo retrieved three glasses from the cabinet and poured them each one. "How are you doing over there, Evelyn. You got enough hands?"

"Yep! As long as you're comfortable with a near-stranger making a mess of your kitchen, I'm doing great."

He chuckled. "I'm totally fine with that."

"Do you have a cookie sheet for the oven?" Evelyn asked.

"Hm." Leo rooted around in a couple of cabinets and then in the drawer under the oven, finally taking out a pizza pan. "Will this work?"

"Sure will," Evelyn said, pulling a piece of tinfoil out of the box and lining the small pan.

While Evelyn shaped the cookies, Leo and Alicia took their glasses of wine into the living room.

"So what do we have in there?" Alicia waggled a finger at the box from the attic.

Leo set his wine on the coffee table and opened the box. "I can't say I'm a huge decorator. I have stockings and some greenery."

"That'll work." Alicia pulled out a long strand of woven spruce and arranged it over the mantel.

Leo followed up with two stocking hangers and flanked the mantel with them. Then they each pulled a stocking from the box and hung them at the same time.

Alicia picked up her glass of wine, stood back, and admired their work. "It's starting to feel cozy in here."

He smiled. "It just needed a woman's touch." His interested gaze lingered on her.

She took a sip of her wine to hide her fondness for him. She liked that she could be herself with Leo, and she couldn't deny she felt alive for the first time in months.

"Do you have presents to wrap?" she asked.

"Yeah. I'll bring them in." He left her in the living room.

Alicia waited by the fire, the warmth seeping into her bones while she sipped from her glass. The smell of sugar and warm butter floated in from the kitchen, giving her a sense of her old home despite the new furnishings. The only thing that would make this night more perfect would be if Dean walked through the door.

Leo returned, carrying a roll of wrapping paper, a spool of ribbon, and a large bag of gifts. He set them on the floor. "I'll get us a pair of scissors and some tape."

Alicia cleared the coffee table, picked up the wrapping paper, and tore the cellophane from it. As she unrolled the paper, Leo returned with the scissors and tape and handed them to her. She dug around in the bag and pulled out the first present, admiring the wooden box with Dean's initials carved into the top.

Evelyn came in and sat on the sofa with her glass of wine. "Oh, what's that?"

"It's for Dad to keep all his photographs in," Leo said. "He has a stack he's kept over the years. I figured he and I could write down who's in them and the dates before he loses his memory."

"It's beautiful," Alicia said, caressing the brass latch and hoping Dean would be able to use the box soon. She set it in the center of the wrapping paper and cut around it before folding the sides of the paper up and securing them with a piece of tape. Then she folded and taped the ends. Once the present was wrapped, she cut off a long piece of ribbon and tied a bow around it.

Evelyn offered to put the present under the tree. "One down!"

The next gift was a brass pocket watch with carvings around the edges.

"Time is such an issue when someone's losing their memory, so I wanted to give him the gift of time. I figured he'd like to carry it around with him. He doesn't have a watch." Leo sat down next to Alicia.

"That's thoughtful," Alicia said. She wrapped it and Evelyn placed it under the tree.

Alicia lifted a sizable suitcase-style container from the bottom of the bag. She set it on the table, unclipped the two latches, and lifted the lid. "Oh, wow."

"It's a vintage record player. It's fully restored so he can listen to his old records. He says the songs take him back in time." Leo choked up as he said the words. "If only I could go back in time..."

"Don't," Alicia warned. "Don't put yourself through the what-ifs." She'd had those thoughts herself. *What if I'd asked Bo to stay home that day? What if he'd slept in like he always had instead of getting up when I told him he needed to?*

"Let's stay positive," Evelyn said. "Look at all we've done. We've got music playing, wine, cookies in the oven, presents, decorations... We're ready."

"I wished for a Christmas miracle at the bridge," Leo said. "I really need it to deliver."

Alicia wasn't sure what came over her just then, but she suddenly knew why she'd felt stronger since she'd come back to Noel. Over the week that she'd been there, she'd developed *faith*. She believed things would somehow work out. What she didn't know was if the bridge had anything to do with it.

Chapter Fourteen

B y the time they'd finished wrapping the gifts and put away the cookies, it was nearing eleven.

"Need anything else?" Leo asked. He'd rounded up a few extra toiletries and given them each a toothbrush and a bar of soap. Evelyn was planning to take the study-slash-guest-room while Alicia would sleep on the sofa downstairs.

"I'm fine, thank you," Evelyn said with a yawn. She fluffed the sheets on the twin bed in the guest room and then climbed under them.

"All right." Leo then addressed Alicia, "Let's get you settled on the sofa downstairs."

Alicia wiggled her fingers in a little wave to Evelyn. "Nighty night."

She and Leo went back down to the living room where he'd piled a stack of folded sheets and blankets, along with a pillow. As she began to dress the sofa in bedding, he looked as if was about to speak, but then hesitated. Alicia raised an eyebrow at him to go ahead.

"There's about enough wine left for us to have a glass each," he said. "But if you're tired, we can dump it."

Even though her eyes were heavy and they'd had a long day, she didn't want him to leave yet. "We shouldn't let good wine go to waste," she said.

He went into the kitchen and returned with the bottle, then poured the last bit into each of their glasses. The house was quiet, the music turned off, and the fire had dwindled. The only lights in the room were from the glittering Christmas tree and the small lamp next to Alicia's makeshift bed. She sat on the sofa and scooted the blankets over to make room for Leo. He lowered himself next to her.

"Thank you for letting us stay," she said.

"Of course. It's been nice. Having you here took my mind off the panic for a while."

"I know what you mean."

Leo turned toward the back door. "I left the door unlocked. I keep hoping he'll just walk in."

"You never know." Another thought occurred to her. "Will I startle him if he does come home? He's not used to having a house full of people."

"He might wonder who you are, but he loves people. He was always the more outgoing one of my parents. He can talk to anyone and carry on for hours. I don't know how he manages to find that much to say to a stranger, but he does."

Alicia sipped her wine, feeling completely relaxed in that moment.

"Dad could be the life of the party," Leo continued, "making people laugh and telling stories. But he's also a gentle soul and he likes to read and spend time in nature. I connected to that side of him, and we could spend hours fishing or hiking. I miss him."

Alicia offered an understanding nod. Were the parallels

in hers and Leo's personalities what made her feel so comfortable with him? With Bo, she'd always let him do the talking, using his charisma to keep the conversations going. But with Leo, they could just be. They were similar in the way they managed in the world. Her grief had swallowed her for many months, but being around Evelyn and Leo had pulled her out of the grief and given her a sense of who she'd been before.

"I'm glad you'll be in Noel a little longer," he said. "If you need anywhere to stay..."

She tried to ignore the flutter in her chest at his suggestion. "Evelyn said I could crash at her apartment."

"Of course," he said with a smile. "Do you have any plans while you're here?"

"I haven't really thought about it. Except for volunteering at the hospital."

He took in a tight breath. "I've been so busy trying to find Dad that I haven't been able to spend as much time at the diner as I need to. I'm not sure how to keep going."

"I'm sure the staff can manage for the time being."

He shook his head. "Many of them are new, and there are still a ton of things to finalize and sort out with the business aspect."

"You're a lot stronger than you think," she said, wondering if she was also speaking to herself. "You'll figure it out."

"Thanks."

He finished his wine, then stood and set the empty glass on the table. He locked eyes with her, the soft mood of the night and the buzz of the wine making her want to stay up longer, but she also knew they should all get some sleep.

"Good night," she said.

"Good night." He offered her a smile before turning and walking away.

As Alicia lay on the sofa in her old home with the same view out the window that she'd had all those years ago, she decided to send a group text to her parents and sister to let them know where she was. She was surprised when her mother responded at such a late hour.

> What? How in the world are you in our old house?

> It's a long story. I didn't expect you to be awake. I'll call you tomorrow and tell you all about it.

> Okay, honey. Everyone else is out for the count, but I've been up reading my book. I only have two chapters to go, so I'm pushing through. I'll regret it in the morning, but I needed something to calm my nerves after all the zip-lining.

Alicia laughed and texted her mom back.

> I can't wait to hear all about it. I'm heading to bed. Good night.

Her mom wished her good night, and Alicia put her phone on the table. So much had changed for her in the last few days. Bo had wanted her to visit Noel. He was usually right, and this instance was no different. She should have come back years ago.

Chapter Fifteen

When Alicia woke to the gray light coming through the window, she'd had another completely uninterrupted, full night of sleep. And while it had been restorative, and she'd slept like a baby, it meant Dean hadn't returned.

The clink of dishes and the rich aroma of coffee coming from the kitchen captured her attention. She pushed off the blankets, folded them, and set them on the sofa. Then she went to the kitchen to see who was up.

Leo was already dressed and stood at the sink rinsing the glasses from last night and loading the dishwasher.

"Good morning," he said when she joined him.

"Morning." She ran her fingers through her tangled hair.

"I hope I didn't wake you."

She shook her head. "You didn't."

He dried off his hands on a kitchen towel and draped it on the sink. "Coffee?"

"Yes, please."

Leo retrieved two mugs from the cabinet, filled them, and then handed her one. "Cream and sugar?" He slid the container of cream her way.

She got a spoon from the drawer and added a little cream, stirring as she peered out the window at the newly fallen snow. Not a single track through the backyard.

"No word from the sheriff?" she asked.

"Nothing. I already called this morning and left a message." He drank from his mug, thoughts evident in his gaze. "I'm going to work on digging out our cars and then try to clear the driveway. It looks like the plows have been by, so if I can get us out the driveway, I can get you to the hospital, and then we can start looking for Dad." He finished his coffee in a gulp and then put his mug in the sink.

"Sounds good. Want me to help you?"

"No thanks. Stay inside in case Dad comes back."

"Okay."

He put on his boots and coat and went outside. Alicia went into the living room, grabbed her phone, and took the folded paper from her coat pocket. She unfolded it and then rummaged for a pen in a catchall basket in the kitchen. She sat at the kitchen table and filled out the hospital volunteer form.

"Hey there, sunshine," Evelyn said as she came into the room. "Ooh, coffee." She set about preparing herself a mug and then sat down next to Alicia. "What're you doing?'

"I thought since you still need to spend some quality time with your parents, I'd get out of your hair and volunteer at the hospital next week. So I'm filling out an application."

"That sounds like a great use of your time. Tabitha Brice is a nurse there, did you know that?"

"Yeah, I saw her when I stopped by the other day. We talked a little."

"She told me the Fergusons need help."

"With what?"

"She said Dr. Mitchell and Dr. Rose are getting older, and they don't run the hospital as well as they used to. It's just getting too much. I'm sure they'd appreciate any assistance you could offer."

Alicia hadn't considered the fact that time had affected the two doctors as well. She wasn't sure she could fill their shoes. "Well, I'm excited to get started."

She finished the form and took a picture of it with her phone. While she sipped her coffee, she pulled up the website and selected the contact form. After typing in a message, she navigated to their upload button and attached the image.

Suddenly, Leo's phone buzzed across the room, startling both of them. Alicia got up and went over to it. The screen identified the call as: "Miles County Sheriff's Department."

With Evelyn on her heels, Alicia snatched up the phone and ran to the door, opening it quickly.

"Leo!" she called waving the phone. "The sheriff's calling!"

Out at the edge of the drive, Leo yelled back, "Answer it!" He dropped the shovel and trudged toward them.

Alicia swiped to answer and held the phone to her ear. "Hello, this is Alicia Silver answering for Leo Whitaker."

"Hello, ma'am," a deep Southern drawl said. "Is Mr. Whitaker available? We've got some news for him."

"Yes, give me one second." She held out the phone as a winded Leo pulled off his glove and took it from her.

They all stepped inside and shut out the cold. Leo's

boots dropped clumps of snow on the rug as he listened. Then his mouth fell open, his eyes widening.

Alicia's heart began to thump and she consulted Evelyn. Could her friend make out the expression on Leo's face? Because she certainly couldn't. But then his lips curled up, excitement filling his features.

"I'll be there as soon as I can dig the car out. Thank you." He ended the call, scooped up Alicia into his arms, and spun her around, making her squeal. He put her down. "They found Dad and he's okay," he said, his eyes glistening.

"What? Where?"

"There's a hunter's lodge in Traverse County across the valley for rent. The back door was left unlocked. He's been surviving on a few cans of food that were left there. He's dehydrated and hungry, they said, but he's okay. They took him to the hospital in Sandston, to make sure his vitals are all in check." He let out a wild laugh of relief. "I've got to get the car out."

"We'll help!" Evelyn said, rushing over to her piled ski clothes and putting one leg into them.

"Go, go," Alicia urged Leo. "We'll meet you out there."

Leo flung open the door and hurried outside while Alicia ran over to the chair and grabbed her own snow attire, putting it on as fast as she could. Once she and Evelyn were dressed warmly, they joined Leo outside. The car was almost cleaned off and Leo had already pulled two more shovels from the garage and handed them each one.

"We'll make a path directly behind the car out to the road."

They got started. The snow was deep, and the work was difficult. Alicia pushed with all her might and struggled to make progress. Leo must have noticed because he came over and jammed his shovel into the snow, crunching it. Underneath a layer of ice, the snow was powdery soft. He went over and did the same for Evelyn before he began pounding the top layer in a path to the street. Once the frozen layer was broken, they could move it a little easier, and they worked meticulously to clear out enough to allow the tires space to roll.

While she worked, Alicia kept trying to process the fact that Dean's story hadn't ended the way she'd originally feared. Maybe there was good in the world. For some reason, Bo had to go, but Dean needed to stay a little longer. Perhaps Dean getting lost and then being found was meant to teach them all not to give up when hope seemed lost.

She still wasn't sure if the bridge had helped. But they could technically be one of those news stories now. And maybe that would give other people hope too.

As soon as they'd cleared a path, Alicia and Evelyn climbed into Leo's Land Rover.

"Hey, I won't be in today," Leo told his manager at the diner while he shut the driver's door and started the engine.

With the phone pressed to his ear, he caught Alicia's eye and their gaze locked in unified resolve. A fizzle of happiness swam through her and, in that moment, she had a stunning feeling that there was nowhere else she should've been right then. Since Bo had passed, she hadn't had any sense of direction until that very minute.

As he explained about his dad to the person on the other end of the line, Alicia twisted around to view Evelyn in the backseat, feeling euphoric. While Alicia could guess how much Leo probably had to do, certainly there was no way he could work. His family had been given back to him, and she understood how incredible that was. She could only imagine what it felt like to know his dad was safe.

Leo finished the call and dropped his phone into the center compartment between the seats. His tires protested against the icy driveway, spinning wildly as the engine revved. He put it in drive and the vehicle groaned, then he shifted back into reverse.

"Hang on," he warned.

Alicia grabbed the handle on her door and held tightly.

Leo hit the gas and the engine growled once more, but they broke free and fishtailed before straightening and moving backward. Alicia was relieved when they'd made it down the long drive and bumped over the final pile of snow to pull onto the main road. Excitement whirred in the air as they drove toward Sandston, the next town over, and Traverse County Hospital.

When they passed the turnoff for the bridge, Alicia caught Evelyn looking down the road.

"You have to wonder if the bridge had anything to do with this," Evelyn said.

"I don't think it did," Alicia decided. "Dean is an outdoorsman, and he had supplies and knew how to survive. Right, Leo?"

"Yep. He could live in the woods for months if he was prepared enough."

"Even though his memory is failing him, he subconsciously knows how to make the best decisions for his survival. He fished, kept moving, and sought shelter." Saying it out loud helped Alicia realize Dean's safety undoubtedly had nothing to do with the bridge.

"You're probably right..." Evelyn said, but the way her words trailed off, she didn't sound convinced.

After driving through the snowy hills into Sandston, they pulled into Traverse County Hospital. Leo parked and they dashed across the icy lot. The hospital doors swished open, and Leo approached the front desk to tell them he was there. He got clearance and they were handed visitor stickers, then Leo led them to the elevator.

"He's in room 302," he said, stepping in and hitting the third-floor button.

When the elevator opened again, they stepped out.

"It's probably better if I go in first," Leo said. "He might be alarmed when he doesn't recognize you two."

"Of course. We'll wait out here," Alicia said.

They reached the room and Leo opened the door just as Dr. Mitchell from St. Francis West was on his way out. Leo nodded to him and continued into the room.

"Evelyn?" Dr. Mitchell said, recognizing her right away. "What are you doing here?"

"We're here with Leo to check on his dad." She gestured toward Alicia. "You remember Alicia Silver, don't you?"

Dr. Mitchell broke into a smile that nearly split his face. "Alicia Silver, I haven't seen you in years. How's the family?"

"Everyone's great," she said.

"You just missed my wife. Rose would've loved to see you."

"Well, I'm here until Friday, and I actually just emailed my volunteer form to St. Francis West. I thought I'd help out if you need it. I'm a nurse."

"You're an angel is what you are. Rose and I could definitely use the help—so much that she dragged me to the bridge to ask for it." He shook his head. "Ridiculous, the things we do for our wives."

153

Evelyn lit up. "You asked for help at the bridge and you got it."

"Fair enough," he said with a laugh. "Are you volunteering here as well?"

"No," Alicia replied. "I'm friends with Leo and I've been following his dad's disappearance. I was actually in St. Francis West when the sheriff stopped by to talk to you the other day. I was going to say hello then, but you seemed busy."

"Indeed." He let out a breath.

"So what are *you* doing here? Helping out?"

"We came to visit Mr. Whitaker. I've been checking in with the police department daily. As soon as the sheriff told me he'd been found, I just had to know he was okay."

"That's so kind of you to come all this way in the snow." But it wasn't surprising. Kindness was what she remembered most about the Fergusons. She didn't know a single doctor back in Savannah who had driven in a storm to see a patient out of the goodness of their heart. Not to say the doctors she worked with weren't thoughtful, but it was different in Noel. It was the way of life in a small town.

"Well, I must go. I've got my own patients to tend to, and we're shorthanded."

"I'll be there as soon as the paperwork clears," Alicia said.

Dr. Mitchell patted her on the shoulder. "Consider it cleared."

"Don't you just love him?" Evelyn said after Dr. Mitchell had gone. "He's the best. I don't know what the hospital is going to do when he retires. He does so much for the community, going above and beyond what most people would do. I don't think there are many doctors these days who'd make house calls or visit other hospitals to see patients. And I think he knows that too, which is why he's still working."

Leo opened the door and gestured to them. "Come on in, ladies."

Inside the hospital room, Dean was sitting up in the bed wearing a blue-and-white hospital gown and sipping a can of soda. He brightened when Alicia and Evelyn entered.

"Hello," he said, his bushy gray eyebrows rising. "I'm Dean Whitaker." He seemed proud to have remembered his name.

Alicia grinned at him. After all she'd been through with helping Leo, she felt as if she knew Dean. "I'm Alicia Silver. And this is my friend Evelyn Baton. We've heard a lot about you."

"All good things, I hope."

"Yes," she said, the significance of the moment taking her breath.

"I went out fishing and got lost," he told her. "I couldn't for the life of me remember our address or how to get home." He recounted his treacherous walk through the woods, how he'd stopped at the small shack and then gone farther into the forest until he came upon the cabin, where he'd planned to stay until the storm passed. "From now on, I'm not going to leave Leo's side."

Leo's eyes were glassy with emotion. "I'm perfectly fine with that."

The staff brought Dean an early lunch, and Leo told him he'd be back shortly and would stay the rest of the day. Then he offered to take Evelyn and Alicia back to his house to dig out Evelyn's car so they could get home and relax. Once they were in the hallway, Evelyn excused herself to use the ladies' room and Leo pulled Alicia aside.

"I can't thank you enough for all you've done. I'm so grateful," he said.

"I really didn't do much, so it was no problem at all," Alicia said.

His gaze swallowed her. "I want to see you again. Promise you won't leave town without finding me."

Her heart fluttered as she looked up at him. The truth was, she wanted to see him again too. "I promise."

Chapter Sixteen

"What a whirlwind," Evelyn said when they walked through the door of her apartment. She threw her keys on the counter.

"Yes." Alicia yawned, the whole ordeal catching up with her. She dropped her ski clothes onto the arm of the chair and fell onto the sofa. After helping Leo get Evelyn's car out, they drove away, and she couldn't help but notice how sad she felt as they did.

Evelyn lumped her coat onto the floor and dropped down beside her. "I think we should get showers and put on clean clothes, and then we can make ourselves some hot chocolate and relax."

"That sounds fantastic," Alicia said.

"Who gets dibs on the first shower?"

Alicia waved a hand toward the small hallway leading to the bathroom. "Go ahead. I want to call my parents anyway."

Evelyn got up off the sofa. "Tell them I said hi."

"I will."

"And feel free to grab yourself some cookies." She went down the hallway, leaving Alicia on the sofa.

Cookies did sound enticing. She got up, turned on the Christmas tree lights in the corner of the room, and then helped herself to a couple of the cookies she and Evelyn had made the other night. Then she plopped back on the sofa and called her mom.

"Hi, sweetheart," her mother answered. "I'm glad you called. I've been dying to hear how you ended up in our house."

Alicia launched into the story of meeting Leo and finding Dean. They talked about Evelyn, and Alicia told her mother her friend said hello.

"You know, I have to be honest," her mother said, "when you told me you were going to Noel, I worried you were going to the bridge to wish for Bo. You'd been so down that I couldn't imagine you'd actually entertain the idea of meeting people. I'm so pleasantly surprised."

Alicia hung her head, the phone at her ear. "You weren't wrong, Mom. The bridge was the original draw, but being away from Savannah has started to help me heal. I can't say I'm the same person I was before Bo, but I'm definitely getting there."

"I'm so glad to hear that," her mother said.

She folded her legs under her, gripping the phone as if she could hug it. "I want to come see you all soon."

"I'm sure we can make that happen," her mom replied happily.

"I know it's hard for all of us to get together, and I should've gone to Florida with you. I'm sorry I didn't, but I'm also glad I came to Noel."

"We'll make time. We need to. We're the only family we've got."

"Speaking of family, what's everyone else doing?"

"Oscar is asleep, so your dad and I are sitting in the cottage with him while Camille and William are shopping. Your dad's drifted off in the recliner."

Affection for her family bubbled up. "I miss you."

"Aw, honey, I miss you too."

"Tell everyone hi for me," Alicia said.

"I will."

Alicia said goodbye to her mom and then got off the phone. A week ago, she'd had no idea what she'd do or say if she was with them, and now she couldn't wait to plan their next trip.

"You've inspired me," Evelyn said later after they'd both showered and changed clothes. She handed Alicia a mug of hot chocolate with marshmallows floating on top.

Alicia snuggled under the warm blanket she'd brought to the sofa from her room. The snow had finally stopped falling, but the chill remained. "What do you mean?"

"I saw how you and Leo kept looking at each other, and I decided I need to try to make something happen with Andy."

"Wait, what? What do you mean how we looked at each other?"

"Oh, my goodness, it's as if you two are already an old married couple."

Alicia mentally thumbed through the moments Evelyn might have witnessed and didn't see what her friend seemed to perceive. "You're being silly."

"I'm not!" She stirred her hot cocoa with a candy cane

and blew the steam off the top. "Tell me you don't feel something for him."

Alicia opened her mouth but couldn't deny it. Leo had been the most real person she'd met since losing Bo. And if she really wanted to go there, Leo might even be more her speed than Bo had been. She loved the way he took care of his dad, the drive he had with opening the diner, and the kindness he showed her even though he was racked with worry at the time. But she didn't know if she was ready to admit something like that out loud. She'd promised herself to Bo and wasn't sure if she was ready to move on. A transition of that magnitude would take time, and she'd prefer to work through it when she wasn't under the glitter of Christmas.

"Tell me about Andy," she said, changing the subject.

"I think we feel something for each other, but we've never been single at the same time."

"What does he do now?"

"He's a pharmacist," Evelyn replied with a laugh.

Alicia laughed along with her as she tried to imagine the high school football team's tight end filling people's prescriptions. "I never imagined him as a pharmacist, but I can't say I can imagine him doing anything other than winning football games."

"He's not as hotheaded as he used to be. He's so handsome... And he volunteers at the animal shelter. How sweet is that?"

Alicia smiled.

"He offered to help me move into my apartment and I've had his number since then. Our paths have always seemed to be going in the opposite direction, but I heard a few weeks ago that he's single again."

"So what are you going to do?"

"I was going to text him and ask if he wanted to get dinner. But I don't want to put him on the spot. Do you think you and Leo could double date if we planned it for before you leave?"

Alicia recalled Leo's request to see her again before she went home. "Sure."

Evelyn let out a little squeal and set her mug on the coffee table. "I'll text Andy right now!" She grabbed her phone and began typing, her fingers moving quickly. She hit send and set the phone back on the table, staring at it. "I did it. There's no going back now."

"What's the worst thing that could happen? He says he can't, right? You're no worse off."

"Except I'll know the bridge has no power at all then because I wished in there to have a chance with him."

"If life was really about wishes and hopes coming true, mine would look a lot different. I think you have to make your own luck."

"Well, I tried. We'll see what happens."

Just then, Evelyn's phone lit up. She snatched it from the table, read the screen, and then hugged it.

"Is that him?" Alicia asked.

"Mm-hmm," she said, a wide smile spreading across her face. "He said yes!" She opened the screen and blew out a long breath as if she were steadying herself. "When should we go to dinner?"

"Ask him if he wants to go after work tomorrow. Tell him I still have to check with Leo."

"Okay," Evelyn said as she typed.

"I'll call Leo." Alicia retrieved her phone from her coat pocket across the room and tapped his name. She put the phone to her ear.

He answered after one ring. "Miss me already?"

Her stomach flipped. "Maybe."

His chuckle on the other end made her nervous. He'd never made her nervous before...

"Will your dad still be in the hospital tomorrow?"

"Yeah. They want to watch him for a couple days just to be sure all his vitals are stable. He'll be home for Christmas Eve."

"Oh, that's wonderful."

"It's unbelievable. Only a few more days of being by myself and he'll be back."

"Well, since you're by yourself, would you want to go on a double date with me tomorrow night?"

"Did you say *date*?" The affection in his voice was evident.

Her cheeks heated up. It had been a long time since she'd felt something like that. "I did."

"Then the answer is yes, of course."

She turned and gave Evelyn a thumbs-up and her friend wriggled in her seat happily.

"Wouldn't you like to know who the other couple is?" Alicia asked.

"Doesn't matter," he replied, "but sure."

She smiled, unable to control the happiness that filled her. "Evelyn asked a guy from our high school named Andy on a first date, and she doesn't want to go alone."

"Ah, fair enough."

"I'll text you the details once we have them ironed out."

"All right. I'm looking forward to it."

"Me too," she said honestly.

They said their goodbyes and she ended the call.

Evelyn waved her phone in the air to celebrate their success. "Where should we go?"

Alicia picked up her hot chocolate and sat back down

on the sofa, covering up with the blanket once more, her heart still pattering from the call. "I don't know."

"Oh! I almost forgot. There's a Christmas pop-up at The Farmhouse."

"Christmas pop-up?" Alicia took a drink of the warm chocolatey liquid, the freshness of the peppermint adding a holiday taste.

"Yeah, that farm-to-table restaurant on the edge of town has totally redecorated the entire space for the holiday, and they have a Christmas menu." She grabbed her phone and pulled up the website. "Listen to these cocktails. 'Naughty and Nice' with rum, elderflower liqueur, and freshly squeezed orange juice. Or how about this one: 'Mrs. Claus,' a blackberry dessert wine slushy with whipped cream and fresh berries."

"They both sound delicious."

"Their food menu is out of this world. And they have horses all done up with red ribbons and sleigh bells. It sounds so festive."

"Let's text Andy and Leo and let them know. Want to go around seven? Do you think that would give Andy enough time after work?"

Evelyn was already texting. "I think so."

When they'd sent their messages, they settled in, relaxing back against the sofa and finishing up their hot chocolates.

"I'm so happy to have you here," Evelyn said. "I've missed you."

"I'd forgotten what it was like to be close to my best friend. I'm sorry I waited so long."

Evelyn gave her a squeeze. "We won't go so long next time, right?"

"Definitely not."

Chapter Seventeen

Alicia and Evelyn hadn't made it through their movie binge the night before. They were too worn out and both fell asleep on the sofa. Alicia had blindly walked to the guest room sometime in the middle of the night and then awoke with a fresh sense of anticipation. Today was her first day of volunteering at St. Francis West.

She showered, applied her makeup, and dug through her suitcase for a comfortable outfit. She hadn't brought any scrubs. After settling on jeans and a sweatshirt, she got dressed and went out to the kitchen. Evelyn was already making pancakes and eggs.

"Want some?" she asked.

"Yes, thank you. Need any help?"

"I've got it."

Alicia sat on the barstool. "I'm excited to go to the hospital today. It makes me feel useful."

"The Fergusons will be so grateful for your help, I'm sure." She stirred the eggs.

"Thank you for offering to drive me over there."

"Of course." Evelyn scooped two pancakes and some eggs on a plate and handed it over to Alicia, then scooted the syrup her way.

"What are your plans today?" Alicia asked.

"I'll probably go shopping for something nice to wear for our date."

Alicia drizzled syrup over the buttery pancakes. "That sounds fun."

She hadn't considered what she should wear tonight. Dating had been the furthest thing from her mind when she'd packed for the trip. Never in a million years would she have guessed she'd be double dating with Evelyn—and eager to go. Mentally cataloging her suitcase, she remembered a cute red sweater and a nice pair of jeans. That would probably work.

Evelyn joined her on the other barstool and they ate, quickly finishing their breakfast. Then they left for St. Francis West.

"I'll be at my parents' house if you need me, and I've got my cell. I'll pick you up at five, unless you text me otherwise," Evelyn said as she pulled up to the curb in front of the hospital.

"Sounds good." Alicia opened the car door. "See you tonight."

When she got inside, she told the front desk person she was there to volunteer. After checking her license and calling upstairs to Dr. Rose, the lady gave her a badge and code and Alicia was in the elevator and on her way up.

She approached the nurses' station and introduced herself to the other nurses who told her the Fergusons were in their office down the hall. Alicia went to greet them.

When she walked in, Dr. Rose stood up from her desk, which was cluttered with files and paperwork. "Mitchell told me you were coming. He stepped out to see about a patient, but he'll be right back. It's lovely to see you."

"It's great to see you too. I'm so happy to have the opportunity to help out."

Dr. Rose cleared a stack of files and more papers from one of the chairs and offered Alicia a seat. "Mitchell tells me you're a nurse."

Alicia sat down. "Yes, I work on orthopedics."

"We could use you in more than orthopedics. We're short-staffed."

"I get it. I've been splitting my time between patient care and administrative duties back in Savannah."

"How many hours are you planning to put in?"

"I'm in town until Friday."

"How wonderful." Dr. Rose's gaze moved to the other desk that looked as if a bomb had been dropped on it—papers were scattered everywhere: admission forms, consent to treatment forms, inpatient data logs...

Noel was a small town, but was the hospital still keeping all their documentation in physical format?

"I know it's not a long time, but I figured with the snow especially you might be able to use an extra pair of hands," Alicia said. Her curiosity getting the better of her, she asked, "Do you have a computer system for patient file management?"

"Yes," Dr. Rose said. "But Mitchell doesn't know how to use it, so we've continued using paper forms." She blew a breath through her lips, her cheeks puffing out.

"Do you mind if I ask what system it is? I assisted with the upgrade of ours in Savannah. I'm pretty quick with it."

"We use VeraPro Health."

"Okay, I did a training on that one when we piloted it, but we ended up going with a different one. I actually preferred VeraPro, but the hospital decided on another model. I could take a look and see if I can get anywhere with it."

"I think Mitchell would actually pay you for that."

"Well, he doesn't have to. I'm yours for the week."

Dr. Mitchell walked in.

"You'll never believe what Alicia has offered to do for you," Dr. Rose said as he dropped another file on top of his cluttered desk. "She can help with VeraPro. I know she's not an employee, but we know her. Could we use her for that?"

The doctor's eyes widened. "You know how to work it?"

"Yes. I'm getting promoted to the director of nursing position at work, and I've had training on it."

He rubbed his chin. "If anyone asks, I could always document her time as a consultant visit from another hospital."

"That works," Dr. Rose said before turning back to Alicia. "Are you up for it?"

"Of course." Alicia waggled a finger at the overflowing desks. "Would it be okay if I organized the filing system so I can enter the data?"

Dr. Mitchell threw back his head with a loud guffaw. "You're welcome to it!"

While this hadn't been exactly what Alicia had planned for when she'd thought of volunteering, she was eager to help solve an obvious need for the hospital.

Dr. Rose set in explaining their rudimentary filing system, showing Alicia where all the documents were located for each type of entry and giving her the file with the password information for the management system. Then she turned to the computer and opened the VeraPro program. To Alicia's delight, it was the same version she'd trained on. She pulled up the online manual.

"So what information is in here already?" she asked, moving up her chair.

"Nothing," Dr. Rose said. "We haven't set up a thing."

"Okay." Alicia had her work cut out for her. This project could take more than a week, depending on the state of the data she had to enter, but she was determined to get it going for them. "Do any of the other nurses know how to use the system?"

"A couple have been through the training," Dr. Mitchell said.

"Perfect. I'll get everything loaded, and then we can tackle informing the staff."

"We'll leave you to it," Dr. Rose said. "Let us know if you have any questions. We'll be down the hall."

Alicia scooted closer to the desk and began organizing the folders and papers. After a couple of hours, she had arranged stacks for each type of data entry, from outpatient and inpatient intake forms to vital logs on current patients. She opened the correct screen in the VeraPro system using the log-in information Dr. Rose had given her. Then she began entering the hospital's general information. To her surprise, she'd nearly cleared Dr. Rose's desk by the end of the day. She still had Dr. Mitchell's to do and then some sorting and cleanup to get all the information labeled and organized.

Both doctors had popped in to check on her throughout the day, and they'd brought her lunch. The work was exhilarating. It was amazing how quickly she could get things done without the cloud of grief hanging over her. The sadness was still present, but the thrill of being around people who lifted her spirits overpowered it.

When five o'clock hit and Evelyn was outside waiting for her, Alicia grabbed her coat and met the doctors in the hallway.

"Will you be in tomorrow on Christmas Eve?" she asked.

"Yes," Dr. Mitchell replied. "Office hours are shorter, but we'll be here most of the day."

"Okay, I'll be back in the morning to work on this some more, and when I get it finished, I'll show you how to use it."

Dr. Rose patted her arm. "You are an angel."

Mitchell came over and stood next to his wife. "Rose and I were wondering if you'd like to stay on with us as our primary nurse, a full-time position. You could see patients, but also help Rose with administrative tasks."

"Oh, wow, thank you. But I have a job back home," she said. "And I'm starting the director position in January."

"All right. But we'd love to have you if you change your mind."

"I'll think about it," she said.

He nodded with a sad look that told her he knew they couldn't afford her.

She waved at the doctors and went outside to meet Evelyn.

"How was your day?" her friend asked when she got into the car.

"Productive."

Evelyn put the car in gear and drove out of the parking lot. "That's good to hear."

Alicia spotted shopping bags in the back seat. "Did you find something to wear for our date?"

"Yes." Evelyn looked over with a satisfied smile. "It was the perfect day of shopping. Everything fit, and I even got one shirt on sale."

"I'm glad you found something."

"Me too. I really want to have a good night with Andy."

When they got to the road with the bridge, Evelyn made the turn toward it.

"Where are you going?" Alicia asked.

"I want to ask the bridge for a good date," Evelyn replied, joining the line of cars waiting to go through it.

"I thought we decided the bridge didn't have any power."

"Well, it hasn't had any negative effects, has it? It's not hurting anything to go through. You should tell the bridge what you want too."

"I already have."

"And how's that going? Have your wishes been granted?"

She began to say no, but she had to admit that her latest ask to feel whole again was actually starting to happen. And Leo had gotten his miracle.

"Well?"

"It's too early to tell," Alicia said, but she was hanging on to the idea that there might be something to this bridge folklore after all.

"It's not hurting anything to ask," Evelyn said again. "We could both use the good luck, right?"

"Sure."

They made their way through the line of cars and entered the darkness of the bridge. Alicia tried to come up with her wish, but she struggled. She'd come to Noel to hear from Bo, but now she wasn't sure what she wanted exactly. A part of her felt as if Bo was already with her somehow, and he was urging her to live her life. Bo wouldn't want her to spend any more time grieving him or looking for comfort from him. He'd always encouraged her to go back to Noel, and now that she was here, she felt he would be happy for her.

Before she could come up with a request, they'd exited. But she didn't mind. She didn't need a miracle. She already felt lighter, unburdened.

As they made their way back to Evelyn's apartment, Alicia continued to ponder what, exactly, she wanted now.

Chapter Eighteen

Alicia applied eye makeup and curled her hair. She hadn't done either in a very long time. She borrowed a pair of silver hoop earrings from Evelyn and then applied lipstick. Wearing her red Christmas sweater and jeans, she was ready ten minutes early.

When she went into the living room, Evelyn was all dolled up in a dark green cardigan with a white shirt under it and a matching green bracelet. She sat on the sofa, her attention on the news.

"They're talking about the bridge," Evelyn said.

Alicia sat down next to her. "What's this person's story?"

"A woman swears that her loved one who passed away guided her to the bridge so she could heal."

The hair on Alicia's arms stood up. Just today she felt as if Bo was there with her. Could he have guided her to the bridge so she could heal as well? Could the bridge have some special place in God's plan?

Evelyn turned off the TV. "I swear, they do stories about that bridge every day. My wish had better come true."

Alicia laughed. The bridge sure did seem to be doing something.

Evelyn picked up her keys and purse. "Ready to head out?"

"Yep." Alicia took her coat off the kitchen chair and put it on.

They left Evelyn's apartment, walked through the freezing parking garage, and got into her car. The snow had begun to melt just a bit during the day, but then it froze as the temperatures fluctuated. Christmas music played on the radio as Evelyn drove them down the icy roads to The Farmhouse on the edge of town.

On the way, Alicia left a message at Fairlane House, leaving her number for Mr. Fairlane to let her know when she could get her rental car. Although, she didn't mind being stranded in Noel. Staying there was proving good for her heart.

When they arrived at the restaurant, they made it to a parking space in the plowed lot and got out.

Evelyn spotted Leo waiting outside with his hands in the pockets of his jeans and gestured discreetly before whispering to Alicia, "There's your man."

Alicia tried the title—"your man"—on for size. Leo wasn't hers in any way, but the sound felt strikingly normal, as if it were true.

"Oh, there's Andy." Evelyn waved.

Andy looked almost the same as he had in high school, just a little older and with shorter hair.

When they reached the men, Alicia was the first to greet them. "Hey, Andy," she said. "Hi, Leo."

"Alicia Silver? Long time no see."

"How are you?" She stepped over next to Leo to include him in the conversation.

"I'm doing well," Andy said. "It's great to see you."

"Same." She leaned toward Leo. "This is Leo Whitaker. He owns the diner on the other end of town. Leo, this is Andy Nelson. Andy was a high school football star and he's also a pharmacist, I hear."

Leo reached out and shook Andy's hand.

"Well, are we ready to go in?" Evelyn asked. "It's freezing out here."

Andy opened the door and held it for the ladies. Leo came in after them.

The wide space was filled with glittering Christmas trees, the old wooden floor a bed of fake snow. The bar was covered in mason jars, each full of Christmas candies—red-and-white candy canes, green gumdrops, red-hot candies, peppermints—and Christmas music played all around them.

"I'm feeling the holiday spirit already," Evelyn said.

They walked up to the hostess stand and she led them through the room to an open table. Every table held flickering holiday candles in reds, greens, and whites. Waitstaff carried trays of festive cocktails while groups of people chatted merrily. When they arrived at their table, Andy pulled out Evelyn's chair for her and Leo did the same for Alicia.

The waitress came by to get their drink orders.

"I'll have the Santa's Sleigh Ride," Evelyn said, looking down at her menu.

"What's in that?" Alicia asked.

"Rum, cream, and simple syrup with a crushed peppermint rim," Evelyn replied.

"That sounds delicious." Alicia scanned the choices and

settled on a drink with vodka, Cointreau, cranberry juice, and a scoop of vanilla ice cream. "I'll have the Jack Frost Cosmo."

"I was going to order that," Leo said. "But I was split between that and the Winter Wonderland Whiskey."

"That sounds good too. We could pour half of each in a glass and share them so we could taste both."

"I'll bring two extra glasses," the waitress chimed in.

"Perfect. We'll do that," Leo said.

Andy set his menu down. "I'll have the Peppermint Punch."

"Okay, I'll have those drinks right out," the waitress said. "And while you decide on your dinner choices, I'll leave you with a deck of our Christmas-themed playing cards. I recommend Holiday Hearts Go Fish. It's the same as Go Fish, except the person with the most hearts matches wins." She set the deck in the middle of the table.

While they looked over their menus, Alicia pulled out the cards and shuffled the deck, passing out seven to each person.

"We should play in teams," Andy suggested. "Evelyn and me against Alicia and Leo."

"That sounds fun," Evelyn said, scooting her chair over to Andy's side so they could view each other's hand.

Alicia set the rest of the deck in the center of the table and then moved over to Leo's side. He leaned in to view her cards, his spicy cologne tickling her nose. She held her breath to try not to inhale his delicious scent.

He leaned close and whispered in her ear, "We already have three matches. Should we bluff and hold them until we have a few more or set them down now?"

It was just a question, but his proximity muddled her mind, and she struggled to process what he was saying. All she could think about was how natural it felt to be sitting there at dinner next to him.

"What do you want to do?" he asked.

She looked up at him, catching his gaze, wondering what was happening.

He questioned her with his eyes, but then a smile spread slowly across his face, as if he could read her mind. "What do you want to do?" he asked again, but this time, the question didn't seem to be related to the game.

The tick of time between his question and her answer felt like a lifetime, their moments together over the last few days flashing like an old filmstrip in her mind.

"I have no idea what to do," she answered.

Interest in his gaze, he laid down the three matches while keeping his eyes on hers. "Best not to wait. You never know what could happen if you do."

The waitress arrived with their drinks, breaking through the moment. The group laughed and chatted about the various concoctions displayed in fancy glassware and adorned with peppermints, vanilla ice cream, and whipped toppings. The waitress took their food orders, and they returned to their card game until dinner came, but Alicia couldn't stop running Leo's question through her mind. What did she want to do?

Before she knew it, they were all walking out to their cars. They'd had such an enjoyable dinner together, and it was clear how well Evelyn and Andy were connecting. Leo grabbed her elbow and pulled her aside.

"It's Christmas Eve tomorrow," he said. "My dad's coming home."

"That's wonderful," she said. "And you have the house all decorated for him with cookies and everything."

His expression lifted. "Yes. But I have to go to the

diner tomorrow evening to get everything squared away for closing for the holiday, and I'm worried about leaving him. I've organized an in-home aide who can stay with him while I'm working, but she doesn't start until after Christmas. Would you be able to check on him tomorrow?"

"I can do better than that. I'm volunteering at the hospital during the day while Evelyn hangs out with her parents, but afterward I have no plans. I can stay with him until you get home."

Relief flooded Leo's face. "That would be incredible."

"I'm happy to do it."

Evelyn called her over to the car.

"See you tomorrow," Alicia said.

With a sparkle in his eye, he returned, "See you tomorrow."

Alicia hurried over to Evelyn's car and got in. She put her hands against the heat blowing through the vents and shivered.

"Well, aren't you and Mr. Diner getting cozy," Evelyn said as she pulled out of the parking space and drove through the parking lot. "I saw him pull you aside."

"It wasn't like that. He wanted me to check on his dad."

"Okay, but the electricity between you two at dinner was so thick I could've cut it with a knife." She put on the blinker and turned right out of the parking lot.

"Really?" Alicia asked.

"It's impossible to ignore."

"How about you and Andy? Did you have a good time?"

"Yes," Evelyn replied happily. "He said he wants to see me again."

"That's fantastic."

"The bridge is two for two. We found Dean, and Andy

and I hit it off. I knew we would..." Evelyn exhaled dreamily as she drove.

Alicia was busy thinking about how the bridge wasn't two for two, but three for three. She'd asked to feel whole again, and she was miles beyond the dark place she'd been in when she first arrived in Noel.

"It was a good night," she said.

Evelyn looked over at her and smiled. "Yes. It was."

Chapter Nineteen

B y midday the next day, Alicia had organized most of Mitchell Ferguson's desk, but she still had quite a bit of data to enter into the VeraPro system. With Christmas the next day, she wouldn't get another chance to work on it until Thursday, and she was leaving Friday. That probably wouldn't give her enough time to train the nurses.

Trying to get as much done as possible, she didn't even stop for lunch, working her fingers to the bone with data entry. She'd texted Evelyn to let her know she'd need to go straight from work to Leo's, since she was planning to stay with Dean. That way, she could work right up until Leo needed her. If she could just get all the information in the system, perhaps she could show Dr. Rose how it worked before she had to fly home. That would have to be enough.

The next thing she knew, Dr. Rose was standing beside her a couple of hours later. "Ready for the holiday?"

Alicia typed in a few more patient status codes. "I guess."

"That doesn't sound convincing." Dr. Rose leaned against the newly cleared desk.

After a few more clicks, Alicia looked up at her. "I was hoping to be farther along with this, but it's taking a while."

"That's all right," Dr. Rose said. "We'll figure it out."

Dr. Mitchell walked into the office and paused to stare at the tidy space. "Wow, it looks a lot cleaner in here. You got all those files into that one computer?"

"Almost," Alicia replied. "I still have more to do."

"Well, not tonight," Dr. Mitchell said. "It's time to close down. The auxiliary staff is here, and I just finished wishing happy holidays to all the patients."

"I love how you take time to see each of them," Alicia said. "It's rare to find that kind of service these days."

"Isn't that why we're in this field? Service?"

"That's why I'm here."

Her colleagues in Savannah wanted to help people, too, but it wasn't the same as what she'd experienced in Noel. The pace was slower, and people took more time with each other. Maybe she could initiate some changes when she went home and got back to work.

"Thank you for everything you've done for us. You've been beyond helpful." Dr. Mitchell pulled his coat from the rack in the corner of the office and handed the other one to Dr. Rose.

"Of course," Alicia said as she shut down the computer. She grabbed her coat and handbag. "Merry Christmas to you both."

"Merry Christmas, Alicia."

With that, she went out to the elevator and outside to meet Evelyn.

"It's sweet of you to sit with Leo's dad tonight," Evelyn said when she got in the car.

"How could I say no?"

They were quiet, listening to Christmas songs on the radio as they drove the short drive to Leo's house.

"Text me when you want me to pick you up. I'll be at my parents'. I left them with the roof of the gingerbread house. I'm hoping they can keep the walls from falling down while I'm gone." Evelyn made a face.

Alicia laughed. "Godspeed," she said as she opened the car door.

"Have fun!"

"You too." Alicia made her way through the ice to the entrance and rang the bell.

Leo greeted her and let her in. "Thanks for coming."

"Of course."

When they entered the living room, Dean was sitting in the recliner in the corner, reading a novel. He brightened when he saw her.

"You look familiar," he said, placing his novel in his lap.

"Dad, this is Alicia Silver," Leo said. "You met her in the hospital the other day."

Dean snapped his fingers. "Oh, yes. That's right." His face dropped and he looked at Leo. "Aren't you leaving?"

"Yep. I have to go tie up some loose ends at the diner before we close for Christmas."

"So why is *she* here?"

"Alicia's going to stay with you for a few hours while I'm at work."

"I actually used to live here," Alicia told Dean.

His bushy brows pulled together. "In Noel?"

"Yes, but also in this house. This was my childhood home."

"Do you need something from it?"

She smiled at him. "No, I'm just visiting from out of town," Alicia said. "Leo's been kind enough to offer for me to hang out with you while he's at work. I don't have anywhere else to go because the friend I'm staying with, Evelyn, is visiting her parents this evening." She reached into her bag and pulled out the novel she'd always used when she was trying to avoid people in public. It looked different now, less like a prop. She pulled the bookmark from the middle and placed it at the front, deciding to actually give the book a shot.

"If you'd like to read *your* novel, I promise not to be intrusive. We can read together."

Her explanation seemed to appease Dean, and Leo gave her an appreciative nod.

"I'll be back in a couple hours," Leo said.

Alicia took a seat on the sofa. "Sounds good."

After a wink at her, Leo left and Dean opened his book, his brows pulling together as he dragged his finger down the page.

Alicia wriggled into a comfortable position and opened her own book. The words that used to blur in front of her began to take shape into phrases, the story behind the letters pulling her in. As she read sentence after sentence, she fell into the story, losing herself. She'd have been totally engrossed except for the distraction of Dean in her peripheral vision, sneaking glances at her. She tried to ignore them, but his curiosity drew her attention toward him. She placed her bookmark in her book and closed it.

"Do you like what Leo did with the place while you were gone?" Alicia asked.

Dean's face lightened once more. "Yes. He's been busy decorating for Christmas."

"My friend Evelyn and I helped him. Evelyn baked the cookies. Have you had any yet?"

"Oh, yes. They're delicious. Would you like one?" he

asked, setting his novel on the side table, grabbing the arms of his chair, and hoisting himself up.

"Sure." Alicia followed him into the kitchen.

Dean got a plate from the cabinet and then took the bag of cookies out of the pantry. He shook the cookies onto the plate and offered it to her.

"We should eat them in the living room," she offered, before taking the plate from him.

Dean followed her back to his chair and took a seat. "He did so much for me." Dean's gaze fell on the presents under the tree.

"Well, I'll bet he feels that you've done a lot for *him* over the years. He told me about the time you hung a tire swing for him on one of your fishing trips. Do you remember it?" When he didn't answer, she added, "Leo said he was about six. And the two of you swung out over the river and dropped into the water."

"Oh, yes, I do remember." The recollection caused a sparkle in his eyes. "That was a long time ago... He's all grown up now."

Alicia set the plate on the coffee table and pinched a cookie.

"Where are you from?" Dean asked.

"I'm actually from Noel originally. We moved away when I was a teenager." Alicia folded her legs under her and brushed a few crumbs off her thigh. "I live in Savannah now, but I miss it here."

"It's lovely—when one doesn't get lost in the forest." He took a bite of his cookie.

"Were you ever scared while you were out there?" she asked.

Dean smiled. "Lost, yes. Scared, no."

"When you were lost, I talked with Leo about you. I

worried that you wouldn't have a way to stay warm. Leo said you probably had matches in your tackle box. Did you?"

"Of course I did. And a first aid kit."

"What if you hadn't found the fishing shack? What would you have done?"

He laughed. "I suppose I'd have kept walking."

"And not knowing when you'd find shelter didn't scare you?" Alicia asked, delighting in this moment of lucidity and wishing she could've known Dean earlier in his life.

Dean ate a bite of cookie and pursed his lips. "Our life paths are like invisible threads that tether us to our destiny. I just had to pray my destiny wasn't in the freezing snow."

"So you think life is already planned for us?"

"I think we always have the ability to change the path, and end up somewhere else, but the learning we're meant to have on the journey will still happen."

Even though this was the first time she'd been in her old house with Dean, it felt as if he'd always belonged there.

"I love to read," he said, changing the subject. "But lately when I try, I lose my spot or I can't remember what happened, and I have to read the page all over again. My outing to go fishing was a result of my frustration from reading that day. I wanted to do something that didn't require so much mental strength. But my ailment got the better of me anyway."

"I'm sorry," she said. She couldn't imagine what it must be like not to be able to trust your own brain. She took a bite of the cookie.

"One day, I fear I will forget everything." He took in a long breath and let it out. "But I know Leo will be able to handle what life throws at him."

"He's a good man," she said.

"He is. He's always been an old soul."

"Has he?"

"When his mother passed away, it was just the two of us. I swear, he managed better than I did. He grieved, sure, but he got his schoolwork done, went to his after-school job, and then came home and helped me make dinner." Dean tipped his head toward the ceiling as if the memory were up there.

"Once, when he was around eighteen, he said, 'It's just the two of us, Dad. We're the only two left to provide ourselves with the kind of life Mom would've wanted us to have.' Until he said that, I'd never considered what kind of life his mother might have wanted for us. I was just trying to survive."

Alicia let the story sink in. She understood Dean's position. Until she'd come to Noel, she'd been trying to survive as well. What life would Bo have wanted her to have? When she looked back up, Dean had closed his eyes. She waited, but he didn't reopen them. So she quietly took out her novel and pretended to read it. This time, for different reasons. She wasn't pretending to be busy, she *was* busy contemplating what she wanted from her life.

The pay raise from her promotion in Savannah would provide a little extra money each month after she paid bills, which might give her more chances for trips like this one. What did she want to do in her free time? For so long, Bo had planned things for them, and she'd been perfectly content following his lead. But she didn't want to follow anyone's lead anymore. She'd actually made that decision before she was aware that was the case. She'd planned her trip to Noel to find answers.

She spent the rest of the evening thinking about her future while Dean dozed. By the time Leo returned, Dean had fallen fast asleep, as if the drama from all the days away were catching up to him.

"How did he do?" Leo whispered.

"Good. He slept a lot of the time," Alicia replied.

"Easy night then." Leo motioned for them to enter the kitchen. "I hope he didn't talk your ear off." He pulled out a chair for her and she sat down.

"He did chat a little bit. He told me that you're an old soul." She grinned up at him as he took a seat across from her.

"Is that so?"

"Yeah. He said you handled your mother's death better than he did."

He peered into her eyes. He seemed tired after the late hours at the diner. "If he had a harder time than I did, he surely didn't show it. He was so strong."

"When my fiancé, Bo, died, I wasn't very strong," she admitted. "It's not something we ever learn, but we're expected to be masters of it when it happens."

"I remember you saying you felt as though you were in quicksand."

"Yes."

"Everyone grieves differently. There's no right or wrong way."

"I understand now what you said about living with the hole that death causes. You don't get over it, but you learn to go on with it. My life can't stop because Bo's did."

"Exactly."

"Your dad made me think about *my* life when he told me you said you needed to live the life your mother would've wanted for you. Our loved ones want us to be happy."

"Yes, I believe that. My mother would've felt awful if I'd

spent my life depressed and lost. I felt as though I needed to have a life *for her*. Eventually, the choices became my own and what would make me happy."

"I definitely get that."

"That's why we get along so well."

A fondness filled his words and she offered him a warm smile. A strong sense of gratitude flooded her, and she had an undeniable feeling that she'd been meant to meet Leo.

"I'm going back over to Mom and Dad's tomorrow for Christmas," Evelyn said once she and Alicia got back to the apartment that night. "Wanna come?"

Alicia took off her coat. "Would it be okay if I stayed here instead?"

"Sure. You okay being alone on Christmas Day?"

Alicia sat next to her friend, the tree twinkling against the dark of night through the window. "Yeah. I have to admit something to you, though," Alicia said. "I wasn't in a good place emotionally when I first got here. But now I have a new perspective. I'm not sure how I got it or what changed, but I just do."

"Could the bridge have had anything to do with it?"

Alicia shrugged. "However it happened, I've had so much change since I got here that it would be nice if I had just a bit of time to myself to process everything."

"Okay," Evelyn said. "I just hate leaving you alone on the biggest family holiday of the year. Even though you've been gone, you're still like family to me."

"Thank you. I feel the same way." Alicia leaned over and hugged her friend. "Why don't I get a ride to your parents' house later in the afternoon—the town bus or something? That way you can have your time with them, unwrap presents, and do all the family traditions before I get there."

"That sounds great."

They settled in for the night, cuddled under a giant quilt, and watched TV until they were both too drowsy to keep their eyes open any longer.

Chapter Twenty

The next morning, Alicia awoke to a tiny break of sunshine streaming in through the guest-room window and a voicemail from Mr. Fairlane, telling her that the parking lot had been cleared and she could get her car out anytime. She rolled over, stretched, and rubbed her eyes. When she peered at her phone screen again, she counted the hours—nine—and couldn't believe how long she'd slept.

Her mind had been quiet last night, but it was back at full speed this morning. She got out of bed, pondering what she wanted to do after she caught her flight on Friday. She knew she'd go back to her condo and the next week she would start training for her new position—all that was fine. But what did she want to do outside of work? She continued thinking about it as she walked into Evelyn's empty living room. Evelyn had left a note on the counter that said to call her if Alicia wanted a ride. She went into the kitchen and pulled a bowl from the cabinet, then opened the pantry for a box of cereal.

She had some nursing friends in Savannah she could do

things with. Most of her friends had been hers and Bo's—other couples. Seeing them was difficult because conversation always moved to their concern about her losing Bo, and without him to carry the conversation, she didn't really know what to say to them. She needed her own friends—friends like Evelyn. Perhaps she could start a book group at work or something.

She got out the milk and prepared her cereal, relishing the quiet. Before coming to Noel, she'd hated the silence, but now she felt comfortable in it. It didn't remind her of the voice that was missing anymore. Instead, it wrapped her up like a warm embrace.

As she munched on breakfast, she decided to call her mom. She grabbed her phone and sat crisscrossed on the sofa.

"Morning, honey," her mother answered.

"Merry Christmas," she said.

Her mother let out a sweet chuckle. "Merry Christmas. How are you?"

"I'm surprisingly well."

"That's good to hear."

"Hellooo," her sister's voice came through the phone.

"Your sister says hi."

A plume of happiness swelled within Alicia. Her family was pretty great, and she hadn't really taken time to notice lately. "Tell her I said merry Christmas."

Her mother called the message out to her sister who returned, "Love you!"

"So how's the tan coming along?" Alicia asked before taking a bite of her cereal.

"Mm. It's all right. More red than tan. My winter skin wasn't quite ready for all the sun."

"I can imagine. I'm as white as the snow outside."

"How is Noel?"

"Also surprisingly good. I can't help thinking I'd rather stay here than fly back home."

"Oh?"

"But staying here doesn't make any sense. I have that promotion starting in January, and I've just finished decorating the condo. I have no idea if there are any jobs in Noel that pay what I need, and I have nowhere to live."

"Sounds to me like you're trying to talk yourself out of it."

Alicia shifted the bowl on her lap. "I'm just trying to be rational."

"Rational can be noble. It helps us make good choices. But you seem so much happier and more at ease since you've been in Noel. You also have to listen to your gut. Sometimes, that voice gives you crazy advice, but when you follow it, you see what God had actually intended for you."

Alicia wasn't sure if she should listen to her gut today. Maybe it was the joy of the holiday or the absolute bliss of being distracted from her grief. "What if I give up everything and realize I've made the worst choice of my life?"

"If it's from your heart, it won't be the worst choice."

Alicia let the words sink in. "Thanks, Mom."

"Of course."

They sat in silence for a moment, and Alicia heard her dad and brother-in-law laughing in the background.

"What are you all doing for Christmas?" she asked.

"We're going out for brunch in a little while and then spending the day on the beach. Santa brought Oscar some new sand toys."

She smiled. "Sounds wonderful."

"How about you?" her mother asked.

"I'm going to spend the evening with Evelyn and her parents."

"Oh, tell them I said hello."

"I will."

They chatted a little longer, then Alicia finished the call and scooped up a few more bites of her cereal, her mind on the little voice that wouldn't leave her alone. *Bo, I need an answer*, she thought. But as she sat there, nothing came.

She needed a sign. But she deliberated over visiting the one place she knew was known for signs. It sure seemed like a lot had gone right since she'd visited the bridge. Should she give it one more try?

Her mind not entirely made up, she finished eating, rinsed out her bowl, and got ready for the day. By the time she'd dressed in a sweatshirt and jeans, curled her hair, and applied a little makeup, she'd decided. She left and went down to the local bus stop. When it pulled up, she climbed in.

"What stop, ma'am?" the driver asked.

"The Noel bridge, please," she said, deciding to get her car afterward.

"Yes, ma'am."

She went to the middle of the empty shuttle and sat close to the window. The driver pulled away from the curb and drove down Main Street toward the fork in the road. After a few turns, they'd made it. He maneuvered around the piles of snow and parallel parked on the side street.

"This is the last stop before I turn around and head back into town. What with it being Christmas day, it's been empty. If you won't be long, would you like me to wait for you?"

"Yes, please. Thank you so much," she said as she got out. She pulled her coat tighter to keep herself from shivering and walked to the opening of the bridge. She stepped onto the path that led to the other side, where light streamed through the trees. With the sun shining today, it was brighter inside, and she could see where she was going.

She leaned against the wooden wall of the bridge and closed her eyes. *I don't know what exactly to ask for. I guess I need to know if I should stay in Noel because, while it seems crazy, everything about it feels right. Could I have a sign?*

"Alicia?" A familiar voice broke into her thoughts.

She opened her eyes to see Leo walking toward her.

"Hey," she said. *Can it really be that easy?*

The corner of his mouth twitched up. "Hey."

"What are you doing here?" she asked.

"I've been trying to call you, but you didn't answer."

She patted her pockets. "It looks like I left my phone on the sofa back at Evelyn's. I called my mom and must have forgotten to grab it before I left."

"Ah, well, that explains it." His brows pulled together. "I have no idea why, but I had a feeling I'd find you here."

Her breath caught, and she looked around the wooden structure. If she concentrated hard enough, would she see angels or something?

"Why were you trying to call me?" she asked, not wanting to admit that Leo was a big, fat sign.

"Dad wanted to see you. He asked for you this morning. Since you don't have any family here, I thought I'd invite you over." He pointed to the wide mouth of the opening in the bridge. "He's in the car."

"I took the shuttle bus here. If I go back with you, I'll need to tell the driver. He's waiting."

"All right." As she turned to walk toward the bus, he caught her arm. "Hey, what were you wishing for when I walked up? Your eyes were closed, so you were wishing, right?"

She peered into his blue eyes. "I was asking for a sign to let me know if I should stay in Noel."

A grin emerged on his lips. "You don't need a miraculous sign. How about I just ask you to stay?"

"Why would you want me to stay?"

He took a step toward her, closing the space between them. "Because my life got exponentially better the minute you walked into the diner that first time, and I barely slept last night because I couldn't stop thinking about you leaving on Friday."

His honesty surprised her. And... she felt the same way. She wanted to stay with him. That little voice telling her to stay was her heart.

Leo tentatively reached out for her hand, and she let him take it. The feel of his masculine grip on her fingers gave her a flutter. He looked into her eyes and she swallowed, unable to keep her pulse from rising. A gentle smirk formed at his lips as his gaze gave away his question: Was she thinking the same thing he was? The tiny lick of her lips must have given him the answer, because he leaned down and pressed his lips to hers. The kiss was soft, careful, as if he were trying not to give her too much to ponder, but wanting her to know that he cared for her.

"I'll walk you to the shuttle," he said. "Then will you come home with me?"

"Of course. I need to get my car from Fairlane House, though," she replied, trying to slow her pattering heart.

"That's no problem. I can take you to get it later."

"Okay."

They let the driver know she had another ride and went

over to Leo's SUV. Dean lit up from the passenger's side when he saw her, opening his door and calling hello.

She waved to him.

"Found her," Leo said as he opened the back door to let her in.

"I'm so glad," Dean said. "I was hoping you'd come back and help us eat those Christmas cookies. And I want to show you some photos."

Alicia climbed into the vehicle, shut the door, and fastened her seat belt. "That sounds wonderful. Have you had a good Christmas so far?"

"Oh, yes," Dean said. "I got some lovely gifts. One is a photo box, which is why I wanted to show you some pictures."

"We've been labeling them all morning," Leo said.

"Yes," Dean added. "It's such a blessing to know they're all dated and identified."

"I've been learning about my great aunts and second cousins. Apparently I have a ton of family I had no idea about," Leo said as he turned on the main road. "I have a lot of people I'd like to meet one day."

"You definitely should," she said.

After a short ride, they arrived at her childhood home. Alicia got out and she and Leo helped Dean across the icy drive to the door. Once inside, Alicia was filled with happiness. Wrapping paper was strewn across the floor, just like it had been on Christmas mornings when she was growing up. A plate of cookies and a glass of milk sat on the coffee table, and while it was probably Leo's or Dean's, it reminded her of when they used to leave out a treat for Santa in the exact same spot. With the tree lights shimmering in the corner, the house felt like home again—more like home than her condo in Savannah.

"Come in, come in." Dean ushered her to the sofa. "Have a seat."

"Want any coffee or hot cocoa?" Leo asked.

"Coffee sounds wonderful."

"I'll get us each a mug. Dad, you want some?"

"No, thank you, son. I'm okay," he said as he pulled the wooden box with his initials toward him, his face alight with joy. He opened the box and began thumbing through the pictures.

"Alicia," Leo called. "Do you mind helping me in the kitchen?"

"Not at all." She followed him into the other room.

"Sorry in advance about all the pictures you're about to see," Leo whispered, making a face.

She chuckled. "It's fine."

"Hours of stories about perfect strangers? Doesn't sound all that fun." He took the coffee out of the pantry and filled the coffee maker, then walked over to her and took her hands. "But spending time with you, even if we have to endure all the stories, sounds pretty great."

She smiled up at him, feeling happy.

"I want you to stay. I want to see you again," Leo said.

"Same," she said. They'd only just met. Could she uproot her life to be close to him?

"I feel as if you dropped out of the sky for the sole purpose of making my holiday. Ever since you got here, I've hoped to run into you again. I even asked for it at the bridge the other day," he said.

"You did?"

"Looks like the magic worked. You're standing in my kitchen on Christmas Day."

"How long does it take to make a cup of coffee?" Dean

called from the other room, cutting through their conversation.

Leo gave Alicia a we'd-better-get-in-there look.

An electric charge buzzed between them as they prepared their coffees. Her mind spinning, she took her mug, warming her hands with it, and followed Leo into the living room.

She sat on the sofa beside Dean and peered over his shoulder as he pulled a photo from the box that showed two men standing proudly against a fence. Dean squinted at the image, his lips pursed.

"I can't remember who these two are."

He flipped the photo over and Leo read the names.

"Oh, yes. They're my cousins." Dean placed the picture on the table, frustration showing between his brows. He pulled out another photo of a beautiful young woman with long dark hair the same color as Leo's, and he smiled.

"This is Maryanne, Leo's mom."

As Alicia peered closer at the woman, she recognized Leo's cheekbones and the same curve of his eyes. "You look like your mother," she told him.

"Thank God for that." Dean chuckled and then sobered as he leaned over the photo. "Maryanne took my breath away." He put his hand to his heart. "Everyone should feel the feeling of knowing someone's inner beauty so strongly that they steal the air from your lungs. Don't you think, son?"

Alicia glanced at Leo.

"Yeah," he said, his gaze on her. "Everyone should."

As she looked in his eyes, she felt that undeniable feeling too.

Dean seemed to notice, his gaze darting between them, a knowing smile on his lips.

No matter how Alicia felt, though, even if there was something between them, she wasn't sure how to make staying in Noel work. While Leo looked through the photos with his dad, she looked on absentmindedly. Her only qualifications were as a nurse, and the hospital in Noel couldn't pay her what she made in Savannah, and she needed that salary to manage Bo's lingering hospital debt.

She looked over at Leo. Had all of this change been some sort of spell? Had the mystique around the bridge and the Christmas season romanticized their meeting?

Or were they bound by the anxiety of tragedy? Now that Dean was safe, and once the holiday was over, would she and Leo drift apart? A sudden fear gripped her. What if she picked up her entire life, let go of her job and took a lower position here, only to have everything fall to pieces? She might not recover if things changed between her and Leo. This was all moving too quickly.

She tried to enjoy the rest of her time with the Whitakers. They chatted about the photos and ate a frozen pizza for lunch while she played out scenarios in her mind. By the time it was late enough in the afternoon that she needed to say goodbye and go to Evelyn's, she'd made a muddle of all the choices.

Leo offered to take her to get her SUV. She said goodbye to Dean and climbed into the vehicle.

The ride was quiet. Were they both thinking about what, if anything, would come next for them?

"I'll see you later," she said when they arrived at Fairlane House, although the words didn't really fit. She swallowed to alleviate the heaviness in her chest as she looked into his eyes.

The corner of his mouth lifted, affection in his gaze. "My dad's caregiver, Agnes, will be here tomorrow. Let's do something after you finish at the hospital, just the two of us. I'll surprise you."

"Okay," she said, her skin tingling with the thrill of seeing him again.

"See you tomorrow, then."

She liked the sound of that much better. "See you tomorrow."

She shut the door and he drove away. She was unable to stop her heart from pattering. Her mother's suggestion to follow her heart came to mind, but she wasn't sure leaning into her inclinations would work in this situation. She dug the rental key out of her handbag, got into the SUV, and started the engine.

"Oh, my heavens, how you've grown!" Evelyn's mother, Fay, said, rushing toward Alicia with her arms outstretched. The portly woman wrapped her in a tight embrace and then pulled back. "How's your mama?"

Evelyn made a silly face from behind her mother, causing Alicia to laugh.

"She's doing well. She's in Florida, avoiding the snow," Alicia said, trying to be serious.

"Well, I see who has the brains between us," Fay said with a laugh, finally letting Alicia loose. "Anyone with a grain of salt in their noggin would be in a warmer climate right now." She linked her arm with Alicia's and guided her into the kitchen where a Christmas spread of food sprawled across the table. "Eat up."

The earlier pizza having worn off, Alicia was starving.

Evelyn passed her a paper plate while Fay fluttered off

to the other room and jumped into a conversation with Roy, Evelyn's dad.

"You'll never believe what I got for Christmas," Evelyn whispered as she spooned a lump of potato salad onto her plate.

"What?" Alicia asked.

Evelyn faced her, her eyes wide. "A text."

"A text?"

"Not just any text. A text from Andy." Evelyn's eyebrows bounced excitedly. "He told me merry Christmas and asked when he could see me again." She handed Alicia the serving spoon.

"That's wonderful." Alicia scooped some potato salad onto her plate.

"It was the bridge. I'm convinced."

Alicia got a ham biscuit from a platter painted with Christmas trees. Could it have been the bridge? "Or maybe it was just that he decided to text you because we had fun the other night."

"Fine, don't believe me. But I know the bridge's magic works. Every one of us got our wish."

Alicia worked to push away the niggling reminder of that morning. She'd gone to the bridge to ask for a sign, and Leo had shown up. She wanted to believe the bridge had some kind of direct line to the heavens and that it could somehow grant their wishes, but in the back of her mind, she couldn't let go of her wish as a girl not coming true.

The rest of the evening, as she made small talk with Evelyn's family, catching them up on what she'd been doing since her family left Noel and hearing their stories of the years after she'd moved, she continued thinking about the bridge, wondering what she could ask for next.

Chapter Twenty-One

After her busy day with Leo and Evelyn's family, Alicia had gone back to Evelyn's apartment and fallen asleep early. The next morning, she awoke feeling refreshed and ready to go back to the hospital to finish the project she'd started for the Fergusons.

When she arrived at St. Francis West, she checked in at the front desk, then went upstairs to their floor.

"Good morning! Thank you for coming back," Dr. Rose said with a big smile, greeting Alicia as she walked into the office. "I'm off to see patients, but don't leave today until Mitchell and I get to say goodbye."

"Okay." Alicia dropped her handbag on the floor and took a seat at Dr. Rose's desk.

She got straight to work and input data all morning. She set up the pages in the system to permit hospital staff to pull information on patients with the push of a button. She implemented dual functionality to allow the data to be pulled and updated from multiple locations to build patient portfolios. As long as the patient was seen at that hospital, their charts could be opened by any department. She input all the staff data, assigning them each a log-in, and set them up with message options so they could converse through VeraPro.

She finished with the system a little faster than expected, so she began to build and save various reports for the Fergusons.

By early afternoon, she needed to stretch her legs, so she went out to find the Fergusons to show them how the system worked. She walked the hallways until she reached Dr. Mitchell in a patient's room. She stopped outside the open doorway out of view and waited for him to finish.

"I'll be back in just a second with a warm blanket, Mrs. Capowski," he said.

A nurse was sitting nearby at the counter, filling out yet another paper form on a clipboard.

When the doctor entered the hallway, Alicia fell in line with him. "Shouldn't your nurse get the blanket for the patient?" She knew they were shorthanded, but certainly there was someone else who could do it.

"Of course," he said. "But they're my patients too. I don't want them to see me only when it's time for their medical procedure. I'd rather they know me as a man first, so I spend a little longer doing things for them, having conversations." He stopped at a cabinet and took two folded blankets from it. "I'll be right back." He left her in the hallway and took the blankets to his patient.

Once he returned, she asked him to come back to the office. "I'd like to show you and Dr. Rose the system. It's all up and ready to go."

Dr. Mitchell paged his wife, and once the three of them were in the office, Alicia started showing them how VeraPro worked.

Dr. Mitchell watched with a skeptical look on his face. "It's hard to teach an old dog new tricks," he said.

"It's easier than you think. See that button?" She pointed to a spot on the screen. "Click that."

Dr. Mitchell tapped the mouse to select the button. The patient data loaded and both the doctors' eyes widened.

"It can sort this information any way you like." She moved the cursor over the various options. "And since I had extra time, I went ahead and built your individual employee portal." She pressed another button. "All the nurses are loaded in. Now if you want to send them a message, you just type it here and it will push through on their screen for them to see when they log in."

Dr. Rose leaned toward the screen and began moving the mouse around, selecting different options, gasping with giddy excitement. "Mitchell, this is incredible."

"It does look rather easy," Dr. Mitchell said.

"I could train someone in data entry before I leave, and they could take the manual home and study it—that's what I did. Do you have a staff member who's pretty tech savvy?"

Dr. Mitchell scanned the room as if he were looking for an answer.

"Toby Simmons might be good," Dr. Rose said.

"Yes, he'd catch on pretty quickly, I'm sure of it," Dr. Mitchell agreed.

"All right. I'm going to text Tabitha and see if her break lines up with mine. When I get back, I'll show Toby what to do."

"Perfect," Dr. Mitchell said. "And tell Tabitha to take her break now. You two deserve some time to catch up. It's the least I can do."

"I'll tell her." Alicia grabbed her coat and went to find her old friend.

At the other end of the hallway, she found Tabitha and told her Dr. Mitchell had given her a break.

"Whoa, he must like you," she said, grabbing her coat from the rack in the break room. "He's as sweet as he can be, but he's all business when it comes to spending time with patients or taking extra time off."

"Well, I got his VeraPro system up and running."

Tabitha's eyes widened. "You got him on a computer?" She laughed. "I figured he'd end up retiring before he ever used one."

"I showed him a few of the things it can do, and he was hooked."

They stepped into the elevator and went down to the ground floor to get coffee. Then they walked outside to take a lap around the hospital.

"How long are you staying?" Tabitha asked.

Alicia wrapped both hands around the cup to keep warm. "I'm going home tomorrow."

"I wish you worked here. No one else would bust me out of my job and walk the snowy grounds with me."

Alicia did too... She enjoyed working for the Fergusons so much. Could she live on a lower salary? It would be impossible with her debt. She tried to imagine what would it be like to step back into her old life after this experience in Noel. Would she slip back into her memories of Bo, the walls caving in on her again?

Toby caught on to VeraPro quickly, and Alicia felt accomplished as she drove back to Evelyn's apartment to get ready for her date with Leo. He'd texted that he'd be done working at the diner and picking her up early, by four. She hurried into the apartment, chatted with Evelyn briefly, and then started getting ready.

"Where's he taking you?" Evelyn asked from the doorway as Alicia fastened her earring.

"He said it was a surprise."

Evelyn let out a swooning sigh. "That's so romantic."

Alicia's heart quickened at her comment. Was she ready for romantic?

"I can't wait to hear all about it," Evelyn continued.

Alicia turned to her friend, thankful that she'd run into her at the coffee shop that day. "I promise, I'll tell you everything."

A few minutes later, she was standing on the corner waiting for Leo. He pulled up beside her, and she climbed in.

"How was your day?" he asked after she'd gotten settled.

"It was great. I was very productive." The time she'd spent talking to the Fergusons and Tabitha had been one of the highlights of the trip. "I really love working there."

"I hear they're short-staffed," he said, looking over at her quickly and then back to the road. "I'm sure they'd offer you a job."

"They did, actually, but I have a director of nursing position back home, and I need to take it. It's a promotion, and I could really use the higher salary."

He nodded and continued driving.

"How was *your* day?" Alicia asked.

"Busy," he said with a smile. "But that's a good thing. It was Dad's dream to open the diner, and I'm glad he gets to see it while he still remembers."

"How's he doing?"

"He's happy to be home. And his caregiver is only a

little younger than him, and he keeps flirting with her." He rolled his eyes playfully. "He told her he liked her hair this morning."

Alicia laughed.

"She humors him." He stopped at the red light. "I left them playing checkers when I came to get you."

"Your dad is such a sweet man. I'd love to see him one more time before I go."

The light turned green, and he continued down the main road. Then he turned into a lot encircled by red-and-white candy-cane flags.

"We're ice skating?"

"Have you ever been?" he asked, putting the vehicle in park and cutting the engine.

"I haven't."

"I haven't either, so we'll be a good pair."

They got out of the SUV and walked up to the skate rental booth. Leo paid, and they gave the woman their shoe sizes. After she handed them their skates, they went over to a nearby bench to put them on.

Alicia slid a foot into the skate and laced it up, taking in the moment with Leo, sad this was their final evening together.

When he'd gotten his skates on, Leo stood. "Be right back."

Alicia put on her other skate and lined her shoes up next to his under the bench. She peered out at the ice in front of her. Only a few couples were on the rink today, which was different from when she'd first arrived in Noel. A lot of the Christmas visitors had gone home, and the next mass of weekend bridge tourists hadn't come into town yet. The lull gave her a chance to focus on the few people who were there. An elderly couple sat on a bench across the platform, chuckling and pointing at a young girl as she twirled in front of them. A couple in the center held hands as they steadied each other. At the far end, a group roasted marshmallows around a massive firepit. The sights calmed her busy mind.

"Here you go," Leo said, returning with two cups. "It's peppermint cream cocoa and, apparently, it's to die for." He handed her one. "It'll keep us warm."

She took a sip of the smooth, chocolatey goodness, the sweet peppermint tingling against her tongue. "This is delicious."

He squinted as he swallowed his sip. "I taste vanilla, sweet cream, and dark chocolate... I'll bet it's a simple recipe." He took another drink. "Dad loves peppermint. Maybe we could try to reverse engineer it for him later. I could put my old culinary skills to work."

"That would be fun."

He held out his hand. "Shall we?"

Alicia took his hand and they hobbled to the ice. She relished his warm grip. His touch didn't feel foreign but comfortable, familiar. No one had held her hand this long since Bo, and the action should have felt strange. Maybe it was just being back in Noel and the holiday season making her feel relaxed.

Leo stepped off the platform first. He stabilized himself and then she joined him. She struggled to get a foothold on the slick surface, gripping her drink in one hand and his arm with the other. After she got her bearings, she began to move slowly with him along the edge of the rink. Soon they were skating with the other visitors while holiday music played above them.

She tried to hold the moment—along with the smell of burning embers from the fire mixed with the sweet peppermint and chocolate from her beverage and the unique scent of winter—so it would keep her warm on the cold nights in Savannah.

To anyone watching, Alicia and Leo probably appeared to be just another happy couple who had known each other for years—holding hands and ice skating with their warm beverages. They definitely didn't look as if they'd met less than two weeks ago. But the thing was, she felt as if they'd known each other longer. Of all the people she knew in Savannah, she didn't know half of them as well as she knew Leo, and she definitely didn't feel relaxed with them. Some people must come into our lives meant to reach us on another level, and Leo was one of those people.

A tug at her arm pulled her from her thoughts. Leo was unsteady. His wobble caused her to sway to the side to try to keep him from falling, but with both of them trying to hold on to their hot cocoas, they were struggling to keep each other upright. Reaching for him, she dropped her cup, and the hot liquid oozed onto the ice as she pawed for him on their way down. His cup flew out of his hand, and she fell on top of him in a lump, both of them erupting in laughter.

His hands gripped her sides as she lay on his belly, looking down at him. "If I had to make you fall, at least I was able to cushion it," he said, his eyes sparkling with humor and affection.

She giggled. "Thank you."

A couple skated around them, but their presence barely registered. She didn't pay attention either to their spilled drinks, the cold, or the Christmas music. In her view, it was just the two of them. And in that moment, she knew how hard it would be to leave him.

"How are we going to get up?" she asked.

Leo stretched his legs straight underneath her, gripped

her waist, and sat up. As he did, he moved her to the side of him. She scooted her legs under her until she was sitting on her knees. Bending his legs, he hoisted himself to a standing position and then reached for her hands. Gently, and still slightly unsteady, he helped her get up.

"You okay?" he asked.

"Yeah," she replied, her stomach flipping.

He let her go and skated over to the cups, scooped them up, and stacked them. He tossed them over the side of the rink into a nearby bin, then returned to her, taking her hand once more.

"How cold are you after lying on the ice?"

"I'm fine," she lied. She wasn't ready to let go of him yet.

He gestured to the firepit in the back corner that was now vacant. "Want to go warm up?"

"That does look very inviting."

He led her to the back area and offered her one of the chairs around the fire.

She sat down, the heat a welcome relief. The wood cracked and popped in the golden flames in front of her as she took off her gloves and held her icy-cold hands out to warm them.

While she thawed, Leo went to a nearby table and loaded a tray with graham crackers, marshmallows, and chocolate bars. He brought it over to her and then wobbled back on his skates to grab two skewers.

He sat down next to her and leaned their skewers against the firepit. Alicia broke the chocolate bar into squares and placed them on the tray while Leo threaded marshmallows onto their skewers. Setting the tray on the table next to her, she recalled her observation about this rink when she'd first arrived. Now here she was, one of the happy ones. She wondered again if visiting the bridge had anything to do with the incredible change in her life and the lives of those around her.

After they'd eaten more s'mores than they probably should've and they'd skated around the rink a few more times, she could hardly feel her fingers. Even the firepit wasn't keeping them warm, so they had to go somewhere to warm up.

"Want to get dinner?" he asked, as they stood at his SUV. "My treat."

With every minute she spent with Leo, her heart ached at the thought of going home. She'd finally stopped feeling awful, and she didn't want to go back home feeling low about leaving Leo. She'd come so far. But she also needed time to think everything over.

"I think I should probably get back and pack. My flight's pretty early in the morning, and I have to drive to Knoxville to catch it."

She could see the deliberation in his eyes: he didn't want to take her back yet. She didn't want him to take her back either, but staying with him any longer would only make it harder to say goodbye.

He opened the passenger door and she got in. Quiet, he drove her home. The unsaid words were heavy between them, but she didn't know what else to do. When they arrived at Evelyn's apartment, she turned to him.

"Thank you for today."

"You're welcome."

As she took in the intensity of his gaze, she'd never met anyone she felt more herself with. Even being with Bo hadn't felt like this. What should she say? See you around? That wasn't true. Should she ask him to keep in touch with her? It just didn't seem to fit.

"I'm so glad I met you," she finally said, the sting of sadness rising in her chest.

Don't cry, she scolded herself.

"Likewise." His jaw clenched, a lot clearly on his mind. "You know where to find me."

"Tell your dad I said goodbye." She swallowed, the word "goodbye" tearing through her.

He nodded.

She opened the door and stepped out onto the curb. With a wave, she shut the door and Leo drove off down the street.

She couldn't help herself, so she stood there and watched him go, wishing she'd said something better, something to let him know how much he'd changed her, but at the same time, not having any idea what she could've said differently.

Then his break lights flashed and he pulled over to the side of the road and stopped. Leo got out and started jogging toward her.

"Did I forget something?" she asked when he reached her.

"No. I did." He put his hands on her face and drew her close, looking into her eyes for permission.

As if he needed it.

Her breath left her. She knew she shouldn't let this moment happen because things were moving quickly, and she had to go back to Savannah. But her heart overpowered her mind, and she leaned in just enough to give him the go-ahead. Leo pressed his lips to hers, more purposeful than last time, and every thought left her mind. All she could think about was the perfection of his lips moving on hers, their mouths working in flawless unison. She hadn't really had any question before, but now she was certain Leo was someone she could easily spend every day with and never tire of him.

He finally pulled back and offered her a soft smile.

"I just figured you could take that memory with you when you go," he said. "And, like I said, you know where to find me."

"Yes," she said, still trying to catch her breath and make her brain work again.

He gave her one more light kiss and then hovered over her lips. "Bye, Alicia."

"Bye," she whispered.

He turned around and walked back to his SUV, got in, and drove away.

Chapter Twenty-Two

That evening, under the glow of the Christmas lights, Alicia briefed Evelyn on her date with Leo and what had transpired just outside Evelyn's window when he dropped her off.

"Everything inside me is saying I should stay in Noel, but I don't know how to make it work," Alicia admitted to her friend.

Evelyn handed her a glass of wine. "The thing about life is that you can do whatever you want to do." Her friend sat on the sofa next to her. "If you wanted to move to Barbados and start a whole new life, there would be nothing stopping you, really. It's up to you."

"I think you might be simplifying the decision." Alicia swirled her golden wine in the glass, peering into it but not really focused on it.

"Why? I feel like we make all these rules around ourselves. But, really, it's all our choice."

"The Fergusons offered me a nurse's position..."

Evelyn brightened. "Shouldn't that have helped you make the decision to stay? What are you waiting for?"

"I have the opportunity to be director of nursing at the hospital in Savannah. And I've taken on all of Bo's hospital bills from the accident. Even though we had medical insurance, the co-pays for his extended hospital stay, emergency surgeries, and life support were astronomical." The prick of tears stopped her explanation.

Evelyn's shoulders fell, and her face filled with empathy. She put her arm around Alicia. "I didn't realize. I'm sorry."

"I need the salary from the director position." Alicia wiped a runaway tear.

"I would love for you to stay," Evelyn said.

Alicia sipped her wine, hoping it would calm her, but it wasn't helping.

"Why don't we go to the bridge and ask for a resolution?" Evelyn offered.

Alicia looked up from her wine. "Do you really think it would work?"

Evelyn shrugged. "It couldn't hurt, could it? And it has seemed to work on a lot of other things we've asked for."

Alicia didn't respond. The one thing she knew for certain about the bridge was that it hadn't granted her wish to stay when she was sixteen. She'd begged whatever powers the bridge had to stay in Noel and received only silence in return. While it was a childhood wish then, it wasn't now. She didn't want to wrap her hopes up in fake folklore, no matter how real it seemed. The last thing she wanted was to think the bridge had some bearing on her life only to be let down again.

"I don't think it will help, but thanks," she finally said. She swallowed the lump in her throat and took in a steadying breath.

Evelyn set her wine down and leaned into Alicia. "You haven't told me why."

"Let's be honest. The bridge isn't God. It has seemed to bring us luck in some things, but in this particular case, we'd be setting our expectations too high."

"These expectations are higher than finding a missing man in the middle of a blizzard?"

Feeling utterly helpless, Alicia set her wine on the table and twisted around to face Evelyn. "What's the bridge going to do, magically find me a job? Drop money from the ceiling so I can pay off my bills?"

"Maybe," Evelyn said, ever the optimist. She squinted at Alicia. "You've been waffling over whether the bridge really has any magic. So give it the biggest test you can. Like I always say, what's one wish going to hurt? Especially if you go into it with no expectations."

"True..." Going in with no expectations was a good idea. But she'd have to force herself not to hope. "We'll just go in there and ask the bridge for what we want and see what happens."

"If we're gonna do it, let's do it now, before I finish my wine so I can drive." Evelyn got up from the sofa and took Alicia's hands, pulling her up. "Get your coat."

Alicia had anticipated feeling a sense of excitement or a tingle of magic after sending her wish off at the bridge, but she arrived back at the apartment feeling no different than she had when they left.

Not having a sign of any kind was a good thing, she decided, because it meant she'd done exactly what she'd gone there to do and that was to send up her wish without any expectations. But still, she knew why she didn't feel anything. She'd given the bridge an unsolvable conundrum, and staying in Noel and having her bills paid off was too much to ask for.

She folded up her clothes and got everything packed into her suitcase for the next morning while Evelyn waited for the dinner delivery they'd ordered.

Once the dinner arrived, Alicia went into the kitchen to dish out their bowls of Chinese food. They set two spots at the bar and sat side by side, ready to dig in, when Alicia's phone rang.

She checked the number. "It's the hospital. The Fergusons might have a question about VeraPro. Can you give me a quick second?"

"Of course," Evelyn replied.

Alicia answered the phone.

"I'm sorry to call you at dinnertime," Dr. Mitchell said, "but I wanted to catch you before you fly home tomorrow."

"No problem, Dr. Mitchell."

"Toby was incredibly impressed with your training, and Tabitha spoke up about you as well, telling us you'd come by earlier, even though you were on vacation. It's clear you have the heart for the work."

"Yes..." she said, wondering what this was about.

"You swept into my office and organized it in a flash. Your efficiency is incredible."

Evelyn caught her gaze and gave her a questioning gesture. Alicia shrugged, having no idea why Dr. Mitchell was telling her this.

"I haven't retired," he continued, "because there wasn't anyone to take my place. Rose and I have been talking, and we don't want to let talent like yours go. So we wondered if you might accept a hospital director position. Rose would stay on to facilitate the transition, and I would be able to step down, knowing the management would be taken care of."

Surely he didn't mean a *hospital* director. Even at a small location like St. Francis West, a hospital director's salary would be *considerably* more than what she was getting from her promotion in Savannah.

"Back home, I'm a director of *nursing*, Dr. Mitchell," she clarified. "Not the hospital director."

"I understand, but we'd like to make you Director of St. Francis West."

She cupped her hand over her mouth, speechless. Evelyn leaned into her view, clearly curious, but Alicia couldn't respond.

"Would you be interested at all?" Dr. Mitchell asked.

Had the bridge that brought Alicia to Noel just granted the biggest wish of her lifetime? The stories couldn't really be true, could they?

"I understand if Noel isn't where you want to be," Dr. Mitchell said when she didn't respond.

That was when she realized she hadn't answered him. "Actually, Noel is exactly where I want to be. I'd love to hear more about the position."

An audible breath of excitement came through the line.

"I'll call the airline and postpone my flight so we can talk tomorrow."

"Oh, that would be wonderful. Rose will be over the moon."

"How about if I come by at nine in the morning?"

"That would be perfect."

Alicia got off the phone and stared blankly at her friend, still trying to process what had just happened.

"So?" Evelyn asked.

When Alicia told her what Dr. Mitchell had offered, Evelyn grabbed her by the arms and squealed with delight. Then her friend sobered.

"Do you realize what this means?" she said.

"What?" Alicia asked.

"The bridge's magic is *real!*"

Alicia thought back to her original wish on the bridge all those years ago. *"I don't want to leave Noel,"* she'd sobbed, tears streaming down her teenage face. *"I want to live in Noel forever with the people I love."*

The bridge had answered *all* her wishes. How could she deny Evelyn's assumption any longer?

Chapter Twenty-Three

By 9:00 a.m. the next morning, Alicia had changed her flight to Saturday, extended her rental car agreement one more day, and arrived at the hospital to talk with the Fergusons about the hospital director position.

"The salary isn't big-hospital pay, but we can offer $290,000 with benefits," Dr. Mitchell said as she sat across from his desk. Dr. Rose looked on from beside him, a glimmer of anticipation in her eyes.

Just as Alicia thought, the pay was still more than her director of nursing position.

"We're hoping the smaller setting of St. Francis West will give you a similar number of people to the scale of nurses you'd oversee in Savannah," he continued. Dr. Mitchell then dove into the job description and the various responsibilities of the position.

After hearing her duties, Alicia felt confident she could handle the job. There would be more administrative work than in her other position, but given the size of the hospital, she'd still be able to see patients if she wanted to.

"What do you think?" he asked.

Taking the director position at St. Francis West would not only pay her more, but it would be an incredible addition to her résumé. And best of all, it would allow her to stay in Noel.

"I accept."

Dr. Rose sprang from her seat and clapped her hands.

Excitement filled Alicia. This was the start of something great.

"I still need to give notice at my old job," she said. "I've got a condo to put on the market, and I'll need to find somewhere to live in Noel."

"We'll work within your timeframes," Dr. Rose said. "We're just so thrilled to have you."

"I'm thrilled for the opportunity," Alicia said.

She spent the rest of the day familiarizing herself with the hospital and talking with the Fergusons about how they handled things. She ran through a few ideas she had and both doctors seemed delighted by her viewpoints. This job was going to be a great fit.

When Alicia got back to Evelyn's apartment that evening, she went into the guest room and called her Savannah supervisor, Katy Woodruff, to tell her about the job offer.

"While I hate to lose you," Katy said, "I'm overjoyed for you."

"Why?" Alicia asked.

"You don't sound like you have the last several months. You sound like you again. Your voice is vibrant and full of life. How can I be upset about that?"

Katy wasn't wrong. Alicia had changed after coming to

Noel. She felt whole again, and she realized she'd asked for just that one of the times she'd gone to the bridge.

"You're the best," she told Katy.

"May I ask what changed you for the better? I'd love to hear."

"It was lots of little things that all added up," she replied, but her first thought was Leo. He'd been there on night one, as if he'd been waiting just for her, and with every second that ticked by in Noel, her future was being mapped out. A future full of possibilities. "Thank you for forcing me to take time off," she said.

"You're welcome. You can fill me in when you come home, okay?"

"All right."

She ended the call with Katy and went into the living room to talk to Evelyn, only to find her friend all smiles with her phone in her hand.

"You look happy," Alicia said, sitting down next to her.

"Andy asked to meet him at Deloris's Pie Shop. She just made a new batch of salted caramel apple pie."

Alicia pulled a throw pillow into her lap to keep warm. "That's wonderful."

Evelyn hugged her phone. "If you hadn't come into town, I wouldn't have been inspired to do something for myself, and I wouldn't have texted him. Now look at us. You were meant to come to Noel this Christmas."

"I think you're right," Alicia said. "And you had just as much of an effect on me. Your positivity is contagious." She was so thankful she'd run into her old friend.

"You need to tell Leo."

"I know. I think I'll go down to the diner and tell him, but first I'm going to call my parents and give them the news."

Evelyn hopped up. "I'm going to freshen up and head out. Want me to bring you a piece of pie if there are enough left?"

"No, thanks. I'll have lots of opportunities to get Deloris's pies."

Evelyn let out a happy giggle. "Yes! That's right."

After her friend left the apartment, Alicia called her family and told them all about the job opportunity.

"You've always loved Noel," her father said on speaker. "I felt terrible taking you away. I kept telling myself you'd make new friends and settle in, but there was always that little voice that made me wonder if I'd done the right thing."

"Everything happens for a reason," she said. "If I hadn't moved, I might not have gone to nursing school, and then I wouldn't have got the chance to work at St. Francis West."

"You sound so confident," Camille said.

"I am." She couldn't believe how confident she was.

Over an hour later, Alicia hung up the phone. She'd had the best conversation with her family, and they'd decided to get together to plan another trip with all of them—including Alicia. With the thrill of the job offer and reconnecting with her family, Alicia checked her watch. The diner was closing soon, and she wanted to try to catch Leo.

She grabbed her coat and the key to the Tahoe and ran out the door of the apartment. She drove straight to the diner. Just as it had been the night she'd arrived, the open sign was still lit.

She went up to the front door and knocked on the glass. Leo's dark form walked toward her. This time, there was no mistaking him for Bo. She knew exactly who was on the other side by his gait and the roundness in his shoulders. She suppressed the smile working its way around the edges of her lips as he neared her.

Leo opened the door, a sparkle in his eye. "Hello, miss," he said. "Sorry, but we're closed."

"I'm not here for the food," she said.

His eyebrows rose. "Oh?"

"See, there's this guy I really like, and I think he wants me to stay here in Noel, and I just wanted to stop by to let him know that, while I have to go home to tie up some loose ends, I'll be packing my things as fast as possible and moving here."

He stared at her, his eyes wide with delight. "You're moving to Noel?"

"Mm-hmm."

"What? How?"

"I was offered a job at St. Francis West that I couldn't turn down. Noel is really the only place I've ever wanted to live, and I feel more strongly about that knowing you're here."

He smiled at her. Then, with a wild laugh, Leo scooped her into his arms and spun her around. He set her down, took her face in his strong hands, and kissed her. She decided then that she'd never tire of the feel of his lips on hers.

"How was the pie?" Alicia asked Evelyn when they met at the door of the apartment after getting back at the same time.

"Not nearly as good as spending time with Andy. But we managed to get an extra slice of the salted caramel." She held out a box as she unlocked the door, and they entered. "And I brought you a piece too."

"Thank you," Alicia said, lifting the lid of the box. The sweet, sugary smell tickled her nose. She took the pie into the kitchen and washed her hands at the sink. "I suppose I need to find a place to live."

"I could call my rental company. I'm sure they have a few open units in this complex. Wouldn't it be fun if we were down the hall from each other?"

A wave of nostalgia crashed over Alicia. "Just like we planned as girls."

"Yes!" Evelyn said, her face alight. "We've come full circle."

"Indeed, we have." Alicia scooped her pie onto a plate, got a fork from the drawer, and went around the small bar separating the kitchen from the living room.

Evelyn took a book of matches from a dish on the coffee table and lit a candle. Then she turned on the TV, and they settled on the sofa.

"Oh, look," her friend said, pointing the remote at the TV and turning up the volume. "It's another story about the bridge."

If she was being honest with herself, Alicia could call up the news station with a massive story about how the bridge had seemed to grant all her wishes too.

"I think the bridge has no power at all," a woman said into the news reporter's microphone.

Alicia set her plate on her lap and turned her focus to the program.

"No power at all?" the reporter asked. "How do you explain the wonderful things that have happened to people who sent up their prayers and wishes at the bridge?"

Alicia hung on the tick of silence between the reporter's

question and the woman's answer. She had been on both sides of the argument for the bridge.

The reporter tipped the microphone toward the woman.

"I think our loved ones and everything we need or wish for are available to us all the time. The bridge just gives our soul a place to put our energy into what we need. *We* have the magic within ourselves to get whatever we're looking for. God gave us the gift of being able to follow our dreams, make that phone call, change our minds... We don't need the bridge to do it."

"I hadn't thought about it like that," Evelyn said.

"I hadn't either."

Was Bo really there, helping her move on, showing her the way? It was true she'd been the one to take each step, to follow her heart, the way her mother had suggested. And now, like some sort of God-given superpower, she knew that whatever she wanted was right at her fingertips. All she had to do was reach for it.

Chapter Twenty-Four

The next morning, Alicia gave Evelyn a squeeze in the doorway of the apartment as she stood next to her packed bags. She couldn't deny how wonderful this trip had been for her, and Evelyn had had a lot to do with it.

"Text me to keep me posted on when you're coming back for good. I want to throw a party," Evelyn said.

"I will." Alicia couldn't wait to get her plans for moving in motion.

"And if you need me to do a walk-through anywhere to scope out living spaces, just let me know."

Alicia gave her another hug. "Thank you," she said. "For everything."

Evelyn squeezed her tighter. "Need any help?" She pointed at her suitcases.

"I've got them. The rental is already started and waiting at the curb, and Leo's meeting me downstairs to say goodbye and help me get my bags in the back."

"I can't wait until you're in Noel permanently." She wrinkled her nose fondly at Alicia.

"Neither can I." The sense of a plan for her life rushed through her, and she couldn't get out the door and onto that flight to Savannah fast enough. The quicker she got started with everything, the quicker she'd be back here, where she belonged.

"Have a safe flight."

"I'll call you when I get there." Alicia gathered her bags and went downstairs to meet Leo, who was already waiting on the sidewalk. The snow hadn't melted much, and she had to dodge a few piles to get to him.

"Hi," he said, grinning as if he were biting back more than just the one word.

"Hi." She stepped up to him, leaving her bags behind her.

"Dad sends his best."

What a Christmas miracle it was that Leo could give her that message. When she'd arrived, Dean's future lay in the balance, just like hers. But they'd both made it through unscathed.

"That's sweet."

"Come back as soon as you can," he said, leaning down and giving her a kiss. "And if you need anything, I'll be on the next plane."

"I might take you up on that," she said, not wanting to get into the SUV. "I'll get everything done as quickly as possible."

Leo wrapped his arms around her. She relished the feel of his embrace as the icy wind blew through them, making her shiver. He squeezed her tighter. Torn between freezing in his arms and rushing to the airport, she opted for the former just a little longer. She'd be with him again soon enough, she told herself.

He opened her car door. "Hop in. I'll get your bags."

She climbed into the Tahoe and popped the hatch for him.

"You got everything you need for your flight?" he asked, heaving her suitcases into the open back.

She peered at him through the rearview mirror. "Yep."

He shut the hatch and came around to her side.

She put the window down. "You have my address, phone number, email..."

He laughed, the playfulness in his eyes making her stomach flip.

"Yes, I got your text this morning. I can contact you in every possible way."

"I just wanted to be sure you could reach me if you need me," she said.

He leaned in. "See you when you get back."

"Bye. For now." She kissed his lips and put up her window.

Leo blew her another kiss and then jogged across the street to his SUV.

A warm sense of joy swam through her all the way to the airport. She hardly noticed the steps as she returned the rental car, paid the extra fees, checked her bags, and boarded the plane. Her book in her lap, she finally felt like she could read for hours again, but instead of grief distracting her, her mind kept wandering back to Leo and all the wonderful people she'd seen on her trip.

When Alicia got to her Savannah condo, she was greeted with a vase of two dozen red roses sitting in front of the door. She plucked the card from the holder and opened it.

I miss you already.
Leo

With a giddy grin, she dropped her bags inside her condo and lifted the vase into her arms. She set the stunning bouquet on the entryway table and surveyed the space with a new perspective. Even though she'd decorated it, the rooms looked like Bo. She couldn't see herself in any of them anymore. Was it because Noel had brought her back to the woman she'd always been, the one before Bo?

She lugged her suitcases into the bedroom and began to unpack, making piles of dirty clothes on the floor and hanging up the ones she'd washed at Evelyn's. She threw the dirty lump into the washer and went into the living room, where she settled on the window seat that overlooked the street outside. All the ice was gone. A couple of people went in and out of the shops, and a few cars passed by. It occurred to her how the view didn't fit her either after her trip. The only thing that seemed like her were the roses on the table.

Bo, if you're here, I do love you, and if you had anything to do with my visit to Noel, thank you for helping me. The pain of losing him and the future they could have had together was still there, but where she used to feel a void, she now had so many things to look forward to.

The silence in the condo still bothered her, so she got up and turned on the TV.

"I knew this would happen."

She whirled to view the television screen. It was just the line of some actor on a show she'd never seen before, but the words gave her goosebumps. She looked around the room and smiled, remembering the woman's explanation about the bridge. *Our loved ones are available to us all the time.*

She blew a kiss into the air, feeling Bo's support around her like a heartfelt hug.

The rest of the evening, Alicia didn't feel so alone. She finished unpacking, ordered herself some dinner, and tidied up. Then she contacted a real estate agent via email and asked what she needed to do to list the condo. Bo would want her to sell it, because she was the one who was still there. It was her decision to make.

Maybe that was what Bo had known would happen—that she'd move on, find happiness, feel whole again. He'd want that too.

Chapter Twenty-Five

One Month Later

After work, Alicia smoothed her crumpled scrubs as she stood in the doorway of Bo's parents' home, holding a handled bag filled with his belongings. His mother, Delia, put her hand to her heart upon seeing her. "Hello, my sweet girl." She reached out and gave her a hug and then tucked her short gray hair behind her ears. "Come in."

Alicia followed the woman inside, the unique scent of cranberry with fresh cotton that always reminded her of their gatherings on his side of the family hit her. She swallowed to keep the emotions from rising up. With every step down the hallway, she walked back into her old life. But this time, she was observing it rather than wallowing in it.

"Bert's still at work," Delia said, referring to Bo's father. "He'd have liked to see you."

"I can stay until he gets home."

They entered the kitchen and Alicia set the bag on the counter.

"So you have a few of Bo's things to give me?"

Alicia nodded, sliding the bag toward her.

A tear slid down the woman's cheek as she pulled out Bo's grandfather's watch and held it to her lips, kissing it. "This was my dad's. He gave it to Bo when he was a little boy and he wore it his whole life." She looked up to the heavens. "Now they're together—no need for time anymore." She wiped a tear.

"I feel him around me," Alicia said.

His mother's face brightened. "You do?"

"Yes. I feel him rooting me on."

Her mother blinked away more tears. "That would be just like him. He'd have given you the world if he could."

"I know."

Delia took in a long breath and produced a forced smile. "So you said on the phone today that you've met someone?"

"It sounds weird, but I feel as if Bo led me to him. I know that doesn't make any sense."

"It makes a lot of sense. If he can't be here to take care of you, he'd send someone if he could. Your happiness was his number one priority."

That warm cosmic embrace took hold once more. "He got you something for your birthday right before he died," Alicia said, reaching into the bag and pulling out a small wrapped box. "I couldn't bring myself to give it to you until now."

Delia held the box and stared at it, tears welling in her eyes. She ran a finger over the silver, patterned paper. "A gift from beyond," she said in nearly a whisper. With trembling fingers, she untied the ribbon and ripped off the paper.

The day Bo had brought it home had been like any other day. Alicia was washing dishes and he'd come up behind her, kissing the top of her head.

"Got Mom one of her coins—a Kennedy half dollar," he'd

said, holding up a gift bag before disappearing into the bedroom to wrap it.

Alicia had continued to suds up a dish, with no possible inkling as to how different her life would become, and how, in some strange and twisted way, she'd end up right where she should be, even though the pain had brought her to her knees before she'd been able to rise above it.

"Oh, my goodness," Delia said, bringing Alicia back to the present. She turned the rare coin around. "I'd been wanting this. I just told Bert yesterday that I might buy it, but at a hundred and fifty dollars, he told me to hold off." She cradled it against her bosom.

Even now, Bo seemed to be looking out for his loved ones.

"Thank you for coming tonight," Delia said.

"I'm glad I did."

Alicia came home and stripped off her scrubs from work. Before visiting Delia, it had been her final day at Savannah General, and she'd stayed later than she'd expected, telling all her patients goodbye. Leaving was bittersweet. She hated passing her patients on to someone else, but knew there were better things to come.

"*You're different*," Katy had said when she'd gone back to work after coming home from Noel. "*You glow now.*"

Over the last month, while she finished out her work days, Alicia had organized her life. Now, after washing her face and slipping on her pajamas, she put her hands on her hips and took in the piles of boxes she'd sorted. She'd parted with the things she'd no longer need, donating them at the second-hand store, and she'd now delivered the last of Bo's things to his family.

But she'd kept what mattered most to her—Bo's journal, which he liked to write in every evening, and a beat-up copy of *Catcher in the Rye*, which he read whenever he was feeling down. He'd said it lifted his spirits every time.

She picked up the items and set them in a box full of other life-memories, like her high school cheerleading trophies and her science-fair ribbons. Then she sealed it up with packing tape, securing her past. The moving company was coming tomorrow, and even though she was exhausted, she still had some organizing to do. It would be a late night, but her excitement over what was to come would get her through.

Her phone lit up with a text across the room. She walked over to it to find a message from Leo.

> What are you doing right now? Did you ever get dinner?

She realized then that she'd texted him after work that she was starving, but was planning on visiting Bo's parents before she ate. She texted him back that she hadn't eaten but she'd find whatever scraps were left in the fridge.

A knock on her door pulled her attention away from Leo's text. She set her phone down and went over to the peephole to see who could be knocking at this late hour. When she saw who it was, a gasp escaped her lips. Leo was on the other side, holding a pizza box and a bottle of wine. She flung the door open, wrapped her arms around him, and pressed her lips to his, nearly knocking him backward.

"What are you doing here?"

He laughed. "You're moving to Noel tomorrow and I

thought you might need some help." He held out the bottle of wine.

She ushered him inside. "Where's your dad?"

"He's with Agnes. She let me pay her overtime to stay with him while I'm gone. I'm at a hotel down the road." He set the pizza on the counter and leaned in, giving her another kiss and taking her breath with it. "Hungry?"

"Starving."

In the bright light of the kitchen, she dished pizza slices onto paper plates while Leo popped the wine cork and filled two plastic cups. He handed her one and looked around the near-empty space, before pacing over to the window seat.

"I could see you sitting here," he said.

She smiled. He knew her so well already. "That's my favorite spot in the condo."

He came back over to her and held up his cup. "Should we toast?"

She put her cup in the air. "What would you like to toast to?"

"To us. In this moment. Tonight is the start of the rest of our lives."

No longer caught between the now and the never, she tapped her cup to his, knowing she was currently between the now and *forever*. And that was a wonderful feeling.

Chapter Twenty-Six

Noel

Alicia's new apartment was down the hall from Evelyn, which she loved. When she'd come back to Noel to do a walk-through, this unit had been a no-brainer the minute she'd looked out the living room window. She was certain it was the perfect home, when from the window she had a view down Main Street and the turn that led to the bridge. It was a reminder of how far she'd come since first arriving in Noel.

She didn't like to be alone anymore. She relished having her friends around. And Leo. She'd told him that.

"I've gotten so I can hardly stand the silence when I'm here by myself. Maybe I need a pet or something," she'd said.

"Just call me. I'll be here in a flash," Leo said.

What began as one day of unpacking had turned into weeks of him showing up at her apartment throughout the day to help her. He'd ring the bell at the crack of dawn and she'd open her door to find his smiling face behind two cups of coffee. Other days, he'd swing by after he'd finished work. His face showed his exhaustion, but he'd have spent hours with her if she'd asked him to. She never did, though, because she didn't want to take away from his time with Dean.

She'd started work at St. Francis West. Dr. Mitchell and Dr. Rose had gotten her a cake on her first day and the whole staff had celebrated with her. And over the last month, she'd felt the same warmth from the staff, with or without cake.

"You're the best!" Tabitha said, dancing up beside her on the way to the cafeteria.

"I hope this is a good lunchtime?" Alicia had arranged their schedules so they could eat together.

"It's perfect."

Earlier, Leo had asked for her keys so he could hang her curtain rods for her while she was at work. When she walked in that night she gaped.

"What did you do?" she asked.

She took in the newly painted white walls and the soft drapery in a muted cotton that complemented the light beige of the sofa that she'd chosen so she could sprinkle navy accents around the room.

He put his hands in the pockets of his paint-speckled jeans. "You said you wanted them painted."

Once her job had started, a few weeks after she was in Noel for good, her unpacking and organizing had slowed down a bit, but she hadn't expected Leo to do this.

He went over to the corner of the room and pulled a blanket from one of the boxes, laying it on the empty floor.

"What's that for?" she asked.

"I made dinner. It's in the kitchen. And since your furniture hasn't been delivered yet, I figured we could eat here."

"You didn't have to do that," she'd said, dropping her bag by the door.

"I know. But I wanted to. I feel lucky every day I get to see you, and I want to celebrate that." He walked over to her and pushed her hair behind her shoulder, kissing her neck, her stomach erupting in butterflies.

There was no denying that he was the man she wanted to spend the rest of her days with.

"I'm the lucky one," she whispered into his ear before he leaned in and kissed her.

An odd scratching sound pulled her attention toward the closed bedroom door.

"Do you hear that?"

A knowing smile spread across his face.

"What?" she asked.

"You said you didn't like to be alone."

"Yeah..."

A whine came from the other side of the door.

"I figured we could eat first, but someone is demanding that I spill the beans."

Alicia went over to the bedroom and opened the door. On the other side sat a curly, red-haired puppy with brown doe eyes, floppy ears, and a giant red satin bow around his neck. "Who is this?" she asked, scooping up the ball of fur.

"Her name at the shelter was Milly, but you can call her anything you'd like."

"I love the name Milly."

The puppy put its paws on Alicia's face and licked her all over, making her laugh.

"I figured she could keep you company when I'm working, and I can help take her out while you're at the hospital."

Alicia sat down on the blanket and stroked the puppy's soft fur, forgetting all about dinner.

"Do you like her?"

She nuzzled the dog's face. "I love her already."

"Your days of being alone are over in every way." Leo put his hand on her face, his thumb caressing her cheek.

As she looked at her new little family that was forming, she knew he was right.

Epilogue

Four Months Later

"The apartment looks beautiful!" Evelyn said as she walked into Alicia's home.

She'd finally gotten the finishing touches complete.

Milly yipped excitedly and followed Evelyn into the living room.

"How did you get everything so beautiful so quickly?" Evelyn asked, reaching down to stroke Milly's head. "I swear I left you still unboxing two days before my trip." She handed Alicia one of Deloris's pies.

"Leo helped." Alicia set the pie down, pulled a party tray of cheese and fruit from the fridge, and began slicing a baguette while addressing Evelyn in the open space over the bar. "How was the weekend away with Andy? Tell me everything."

Evelyn melted into the leather sofa in a swoony lump and put her wrist on her forehead. "It was incredible. We spent a day at the spa in New York getting couples' massages. Then he took me to dinner at this stunning restaurant where we had filet and champagne. We slept in, and then walked all around the city. When we got tired, he paid for a carriage ride, and we spent the rest of the day talking and laughing. He's so wonderful."

Alicia brought the tray over to the coffee table, scooting it far enough to be out of Milly's reach. "I'm so happy for you."

Evelyn jumped up and grabbed Alicia's arm. "Before we left, he took me into Tiffany's."

Alicia gawked at her. "To window-shop?"

Evelyn shook her head and waved her hand, showing off a sparkly ring. "It's a promise ring."

"Oh, my gosh!" Alicia plowed into her friend with a hug, nearly knocking her over, the two of them wobbling and giggling.

"He gave it to me right there in the store."

Alicia clapped a hand over her mouth, delighted for her friend.

The doorbell rang, distracting them. Alicia opened the door to find Andy holding a bottle of white wine.

"Get in here!" She grabbed the lapel of his coat and dragged him into the living room. "Evelyn just showed me some jewelry that was purchased over the weekend."

Andy's face reddened before he handed her the wine. "Happy housewarming."

"Thank you," Alicia said, accepting the bottle.

While she tugged the cork, the doorbell rang again, and Evelyn let in Leo and Dean.

"You're just in time for a toast," Alicia called hello to Leo before giving the cork another tug, the wine opening with an airy pop when she got it loose.

Leo came over to her, set a bouquet of flowers on the counter, and gave her a kiss before cuddling Milly, who was overjoyed to see him, her tail wagging furiously.

Alicia picked up the bouquet and took in the scents of lilac and rose. "These are beautiful, thank you."

"Of course."

"We're celebrating," she said, filling the stemware she'd set out.

"Oh?" Leo asked.

"Andy and Evelyn are exclusive. He gave her a promise ring," she told him as she pulled a vase from under the counter and filled it with water. She unwrapped the bouquet and placed the flowers into the vase, the bright colors giving the kitchen a vibrance it hadn't had before.

On the other side of the bar, Evelyn was already showing her ring to Dean as he sat in a chair across from the fireplace. "Double-date time!" she called over her shoulder.

Alicia slid the glasses of wine to the edge of the counter to take them into the living room. Leo stood behind her and put his arms around her waist.

"How long did you say I have to wait before you'll consider taking the next step with me?" he asked into her ear, making her laugh.

"I want to be sure I'm standing on my own two feet first. And we don't want to rush it."

"Why not?" He nibbled her ear. "I already know what I want."

She abandoned the wine and turned toward him, his hands pinning her to the counter. He pressed his lips to hers, their warmth still taking her breath away. Then he pulled back, his gaze swallowing her.

"I'm monopolizing you and you have guests."

"Yes," she said, but she didn't try to move. She could've stayed in his eyes the rest of the night.

After a moment, she handed him two glasses and then poured a few more. "The Fergusons should be here any minute. And Tabitha is coming... Dean, do you want any wine?"

"Just a little," he said as the puppy sniffed his shoes.

Alicia and Leo took the glasses into the living room and handed them out.

"Before everyone gets here, I'd like to propose a toast," she said. "To love." She raised her glass. She stopped to take in the coziness of the peppermint scent from her candles, the firelight, and her favorite people around her. She peered past them to the turn where the bridge sat waiting for the next wish. Life could certainly be hard, but the difficult times had made her appreciate what she had so much more. She knew she wouldn't need the bridge ever again. Maybe there would be more hard times, but she had wonderful friends and family to get her through.

She couldn't imagine a more perfect future.

A Letter from Jenny

Hello!

Thank you so much for picking up my novel, *The Noel Bridge*. I hope this story has you believing in the magical power of love and made you feel all Christmassy.

If you'd like to know when my next book is coming out, you can sign up for new Harpeth Road release alerts here:

www.harpethroad.com/jenny-hale-newsletter-signup

I won't share your information with anyone else, and I'll only email you a quick message when new books go on sale.

If you enjoyed *The Noel Bridge*, I'd be so thankful if you'd write a review online. Seeing feedback from readers helps persuade others to pick up my book for the first time. It's one of the biggest gifts you could give me.

Until next time,
    Jenny

Acknowledgments

I have to thank Oliver Rhodes who got me here. He saw my raw talent, knew just how to build upon it, and set the bar for everything I do with Harpeth Road. A mentor in every part of my career, he's the reason you have books to read from me and Harpeth Road Press.

I could not bring this book to readers without my amazing editors: Karli Jackson, who is the master of story development; the fabulous Jodi Hughes, who I truly believe is one of the best line editors in the business; Lauren Finger, my copyeditor extraordinaire, who I absolutely adore; the most wonderful proofreader, Charlotte Hayes-Clemens; and Harpeth Road's intern Randi Smith for her final sweep (and a few great catches). I couldn't have had a better team for this novel.

The wonderfully talented Kristen Ingebretson, my cover designer, is the best of the best. Working with her on concepts is one of my favorite parts of the process. I'm so very thankful to have her for cover direction.

Thank you to Kathy Kunclrs Hernandez for tidying up my in-flight storyline!

And, most importantly, thank you to my husband, Justin, who is always cheering me on and letting me lead the way with every crazy idea I have. I couldn't do it without him.